Sell Yourself a Smile

Poems About
the Smiles of Life

Barbara Welsh

ILLUSTRATED BY Catharine Mannion

Cover Design, Typography & Production by Hallard Press LLC
Illustrations: Donna Yankus (background), Catharine Mannion (illustration)

Published by Hallard Press LLC.
www.HallardPress.com   Info@HallardPress.com   352-234-6099
Bulk copies of this book can be ordered at Info@HallardPress.com

Publisher's Cataloging-in-Publication data

Names: Welsh, Barbara C., author. | Mannion, Catherine, illustrator.
Title: Sell yourself a smile: poems about the smiles of life / by Barbara C. Welsh; illustrated by Catherine Mannion.
Description: The Villages, FL: Hallard Press LLC, 2023.
Identifiers: LCCN: 2023913394 | ISBN: 978-1-951188-93-1 (Print) ISBN: 978-1-951188-94-8 (Ebook)
Subjects: LCSH Poetry, American. | BISAC POETRY / American / General | POETRY / Subjects & Themes / Family | POETRY / Women Authors
Classification: LCC PS3623.E4825 O54 2022 | DDC 811.6--dc23

Printed in the United States of America   1

ISBN: 978-1-951188-93-1 (Paperback)
ISBN: 978-1-951188-94-8 (Ebook)

DEDICATION

The book is dedicated to my terrific husband Michael Yankus. He is always there for me and helps in so many different and special ways. He is my hero, my friend, and my protector.

Smiles 5¢

Table of Contents

Sell Yourself a Smile

FOREWORD

By Barbara Romine, PhD
Former Professor of Literature, Language, and Writing
at Georgia Southern University, and Centre College

Barbara Welsh and I have been truly great friends since college, a long time; and even though we live in different parts of the country we get together when life allows. She discovered her talent for writing poetry during the Covid19 pandemic when we all feared for our lives, were afraid to go outside, be near others, or hug someone. Instead of just fretting about it, Barbara picked up her pen and began to write poems about love, kindness, and caring for one another. She published her first book of poems entitled *One Bright Day* in 2022 and is quickly becoming a notable, prolific poet of our time.

In her new book, *Sell Yourself a Smile,* Barbara uses every human emotion to capture her love for others, life's experiences and her spirituality to write poetry that will refresh and restore your heart.

Her poems "A Shoulder to Cry On" and "Follow Truth" reflect the kind of friend Barbara has been to me and others.

Dancing is one of Barbara's passions. I believe the language, interpretation, movement, meditation, and concentration learned from dance is now intrinsic and complements her poetry. Interpreting music with dance enhances her ability to write truly inspirational, lyrical poems such as "Language of Dancing" and "Better When I'm Dancing." You will find references to music and dance throughout. In fact, there's a chapter entitled High on Dancing!

Barbara's depth of knowledge, thought, and wisdom about life and its truths and consequences are irreproachable and offer tips and solutions that readers will find invaluable. Wise words about relationships, faith, family, happiness, peace, forgiveness, fear, truth, friendship, bravery, and heartbreak pour out of her into her poems.

Readers will find funny poems ("Opal and Earl Pickle"and "Bumps and Lumps"), poems about animals ("Morning Fishing"), and even poems about eating your vegetables ("Who Hates Brussels Sprouts"), along with poetry about the Christian faith that sustains her in "A Rough and Rocky Road" and "Faith to Move a Mountain."

Barbara Welsh's second book of poems, *Sell Yourself a Smile*, is full of encouraging tips and words that poetry lovers will want to add to their collections and share with everyone they know.

OTHER BOOKS BY BARBARA WELSH

One Bright Day
Poems about the Dances of Life
Illustrated by Donna Yankus

Sell Yourself a Smile
Poems About the Smiles of Life
Illustrated by Catharine Mannion

Chapter 1:

Eat Your Vegetables

Pick a Pack of Peppers

Nutritious, sweet and ready to eat
A red pepper can serve as a treat.
Bell peppers are classified as a fruit.
They grow from a flower and are not a root.
Red peppers are vibrant and bright.
Chopped, diced or sliced they taste just right.
They pack the most flavor and are nutritionally best
Because they stay on the vine longer than the rest.
Bell peppers can be eaten raw or with a dip,
Definitely healthier than eating potato chips.
They're available in red, green, orange, and yellow.
Ground into paprika they become a spice that's mellow.
There are other peppers that aren't sweet like berries
They challenge the taste buds with the punch they carry.
Peppers can be sweet, spicy, mild or hot
Add them to your diet, there's no reason not.

Watermelon Radishes

I think I could become a true vegetarian
To ensure that I'm healthy when an octogenarian.
I love white, orange and purple sweet potatoes
And cherry, grape, beefsteak and roma tomatoes.

I love all sorts of vegetables because they are so nutritious
But also when served as a meal they are very delicious.
Picked right from the garden and onto the plate
Eat them when fresh before it's too late.

There are so many veggies I didn't know even exist
Served plain, salted or sprinkled with cheese for a twist.
Cultivated and grown more scientifically these days
Hydroponics and vertical gardens are new creative ways.

Controlling the temperature, amount of water and light
Produces a flavorful product for our dining delight.
Micro greens are picked when the first leaves are young
Healthy and nutritious so why not try them just for fun.

Arugula, beets, broccoli, rainbow chard micro greens are
    just a few
And kale, purple kohlrabi, and radish seem very new.
Sugar snap peas, herbs and collard greens
Will keep you healthy and surprisingly lean.
I also discovered a vegetable that's very unique but oh
    what a treat
A watermelon radish is a nice salad addition, but don't
    expect it to be sweet.
It tastes somewhat spicy and looks like a watermelon when
    sliced
The red and green colors add to a salad when chopped up
    or diced.

A watermelon radish may be something very new to you
Don't be reluctant to try it because you may like it too.
So my motto is to eat some vegetables every day
And you will stay healthy and keep the doctor away.

Green Pigeon Peas

Last night I had something new as a side dish for dinner
I was reluctant to try but it became quite a winner.
I needed a green vegetable so opened the can
Of green pigeon peas and heated them in a pan.

In Spanish I believe they are called grandules verdes
High in protein and fiber to stay healthy and sturdy.
It all started when I went to the grocery store
For some Goya products I had not tried them before.

Goya has a long-standing history of donating food in times
 of disaster
Sent directly to charities and the homeless to make it much
 faster.
They donate millions of dollars of their products to food
 banks each year
They share an altruistic concern for the needy it's quite
 clear.

Goya made over 20,000 masks for the recent pandemic
But many say all these statistics and good deeds are non
 academic.
People are sometimes so hard to figure out
They seem to act before thinking of the consequences no
 doubt.

Why stop buying a company's products that does so much
  good
I said to myself maybe I misunderstood.
I recommend pigeon peas because they they taste delicious
Just like black beans, red beans and chick peas they're also
  nutritious.

Visit your favorite market, check out all the Goya products
  on the shelf
You'll be surprised at the variety of products to enjoy for
  yourself.
You may also want to try beverages, seasonings, and sauces
  as a treat
They even have black bean burgers for those who don't eat
  meat.

The Bathroom Scale

Is the bathroom scale your friend or foe —
Some days yes and some days no?
What it reveals can make your day
Or cause you to want to run away.
Whether the number goes up or down
Smile anyway even if you want to frown.
Daily weighing may cause discouragement
That could lead to your malnourishment.
But if you crave feedback and control,
It may help you to reach your goal.
Daily fluctuations are part of the game,
When there's more than one thing to blame.
Avoid letting a number serve as a slave
So you are tempted to misbehave.
Cues other than the reading on a scale
Should be the main concerns that prevail.
Staying healthy, looking snappy,
Enjoying life and feeling happy
Are more important than what you weigh
Your family, friends and God love you anyway.

Who Hates Brussels Sprouts?

Who wouldn't hate them
And be quick to condemn?
They're green and slimy,
Sometimes rather putrid and moldy.
While cooking they have a horrible smell
Apart from that, I think they're really swell.
Brussels sprouts are like little cabbages with edible buds
Maybe you can rinse away the strong taste with a lot of
	suds.
They contain a chemical causing a bitterness that is
	unforeseen
Did you know this taste occurs only to people with a
	certain gene?
Surprisingly, it could be in your genes that determines your
	feelings
About these controversial vegetables and any of your
	dealings.
Some people try to conceal their pungency with other
	ingredients
But do you think that going to all this trouble is really very
	expedient?
With over 20,000 species of edible plants in which to
	diversify
Absolutely, you can hate Brussels sprouts without having
	to explain why.

Chapter 2:

Animal Buddies

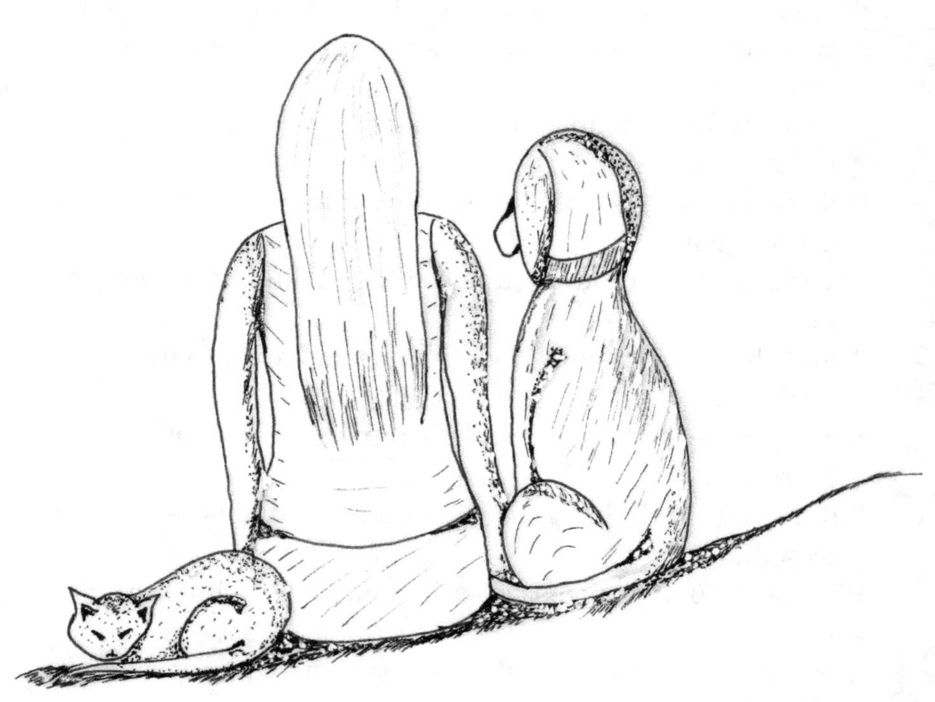

Morning Fishing

Snowy white egrets are seen on a Florida lake each morn
Evenly spaced as if they are getting ready to perform
Around the lake scoping out the water with focused eyes
Searching for a fish to find as their prize.
A fight often ensues and wings go flapping
Trying to steal another's fish by attacking.
Egrets wade in the water looking for fish
As their long legs glide along as they swish.
Observing egrets on a lake provides a unique show
When we take time to embrace the sun's warming glow
And watch each day end as the sun sets and nature sleeps
Until egrets wake to see what today's morning fishing
    reaps.

One Lone Duck

Is it bad luck
If there's only one duck
Floating on the lake today?
As the wind blows he doesn't sway
He moves swiftly with the current
The light rain falling is not a deterrent
Because of his waterproof feathers
And webbed feet that serve as propellers.
God provides a duck with all he needs to survive.
The lake contains all the food on which he can thrive.
He dives for a fish, swimming underwater achieving his
    purpose
To capture dinner traveling several feet before he will
    resurface.
Small fish, insects and worms are part of his diet
He whistles and coos and doesn't stay quiet.
He looks yonder calling for his friends to appear
They soon will join him flocking together as you hear
A symphony of ducks and birds singing in harmony all in a
    pack
They gather cooperatively on the lake making it hard to
    keep track.
These gregarious creatures of nature are part of God's plan
Awesome in power He cares for one lone duck the same as
    for all of man.

Buddies for Life

Pets and little kids have a unique awareness;
They treat each person with equal fairness.
Tenderness and kindness carries them a long way;
Feeling loved throughout each night and every day.
When necessary, they exhibit a strong fighter spirit;
Like underdogs who beat the odds and don't want the
    credit.
They become a family's unifying factor in so many ways,
By enjoying the simple things in life without having a say.
Happiness surrounds them when given enough attention;
Their enthusiasm is contagious adding a bright new
    dimension.
They strike a chord with your heart strings whenever they
    are near;
Unconditional love is a two-way street as it eventually does
    appear.
Animals can join loving hearts together with their
    presence;
As a part of the family, winsomeness constitutes their
    essence.
They give the home a spark of energy and increased
    liveliness,
As close bonds are forming, there is a feeling of
    peacefulness.
Pets are always ready to adapt to any situation they face,
By giving and receiving an affectionate and protective
    embrace.
Eventually you and your pet become buddies for life;
Just like a new baby, they produce a feeling of unplanned
    delight.

The Friendly Red Cardinals

Red cardinals bring life and color, and give us hope.
Their bright red color is part of nature's kaleidoscope.
The sight of a cardinal is an uplifting and happy sign.
They are easy to spot because of their flashy design.

They may evoke an emotional or spiritual feeling.
The male's scarlet red plumage is very appealing;
Majestic with their long tails and crested heads
Bringing forth a brilliant spectacle of the color red.

Carol and Ken look forward each year to Spring
Enabling them to spot the beautiful red cardinals that it brings.
The cardinals nestle in the same palm tree in their yard
    every year.
It welcomes them home where they live safely without fear.

Two years ago in April there appeared a little red baby bird
Hiding in the rose bush indicating something special had
    occurred.
Its mama and papa were in the palm tree about ten feet away
Keeping guard over their baby making sure it was okay.

They flew in and out feeding their baby ensuring it was
    free from harm
The baby grew and became playful looking like a tiny red
    charm.
Young baby cardinals are known to be pretty demanding—
In the first days after they hatch it is quite outstanding.

A mama bird feeds her baby about eight times an hour!
In the aviary world, the mama bird is a genuine
    superpower.
Finally able to spread its wings, the baby bird flies here
    and there
As mama and poppa swoop back and forth to offer care.

Like all parents, they are always around for protection
To teach and provide guidance and direction.
Today Carol saw one of the cardinals on the lower branch
  of the palm tree.
Perhaps a new baby will appear this year; she'll have to
  wait and see.

Cardinals may show up any place where there's dense low
  cover,
Such as lush backyards and palm trees as Carol and Ken
  did discover.
They listen to the cardinals sing their pleasant songs
While other birds sometimes sing along.

Carol listens and recalls cherished memories of times past.
The songs remind her of the love for her family that will
  always last.
Carol has discovered that cardinals are lively, bright and
  amazing songsters.
They are beloved for their beauty often serving as mood
  enhancers.

Carol and Ken's story reflects how life changes for all
  mothers and fathers.
As seasons change, a new baby may arrive as older ones
  blossom.
Their lives are turned upside down to keep each new baby
  alive;
Existing to nourish and cultivate their babies insuring they
  will thrive.

Like cardinals, we depend on instincts to learn how to give
  love;
To care for others with guidance that comes from above.
God oversees and orchestrates our future and remains in
  control
Helping to maintain peace in our homes and delight in our
  souls.

The Fragility of Life

The monarch butterfly is a wonder of nature
As an endangered species we must be crusaders
In order to protect and help save from extinction—
These delicate beauties with their yellow-orange wings of
　distinction.
If you study caterpillars you will discover all about these
　remarkable creatures.
The milkweed or American tiger butterfly is known for its
　vibrant features.
The development of these fabulous creations is a metaphor
For our own lives and all living beings that have come
　before.
Raising caterpillars generates new experiences each season
Representative of rebirth, change, hope and marvel as
　reasons
That butterfly enthusiasts faithfully observe and follow the
　process
Feeling empathy as they intensely monitor the butterfly's
　progress.
Their magnificent but short life closely mirrors spiritual
　transformation
Helping to realize that life and time on this earth is limited
　in duration.
We can only begin to comprehend the vulnerability and
　fragility of life
And see that all living things serve a purpose in God's truly
　perfect design.

Worries and Wombats

Do you lie awake at night worrying about wombats?
Better than worrying about voting for who, this and that
What? You say, why would I worry about a wombat?
Instead, I should worry more about all these ding bats.
Wombats are short-legged marsupials
Mammals who are mainly quite peaceful.
After birth, they develop and are carried safely
In their mom's backward-facing pouch.
Muscular in nature and never considered a slouch.
If you go to Australia you may see one of these
Usually nocturnal so there are no guarantees.
Losing sleep over something you can't control
Like wombats, ding bats, marsupials and all that junk
You need to clear your head and get out of your funk
Ask God for peace of heart and mind
Leaving all your questions and troubles behind
Erase worries about wombats and other such fears
Replace them with faith to dry away all of your tears
God carries us in His pouch of protection to keep away
   harm
Content like a baby wombat, we fit like a cherished charm
We're blessed with a heavenly Father who loves us
He carries and protects us through good times and bad
You have been chosen so give thanks, be glad and not sad.

Chestnut the Sea Turtle

An Aquarium is a fascinating place to explore the sea and
    all its wonders
Committed to preserving and protecting marine life, not to
    be put asunder.
A rescue center at an aquarium is dedicated to the
    rehabilitation and release
Of seals, sea turtles, whales, dolphins and porpoises all
    critically endangered
Facing the real threat of extinction hoping that these
    dangers will decrease.

At the Long Island aquarium rescue center, I noticed an
    unusual sea turtle
I found out her name is Chestnut, although I wanted to call
    her Miss Myrtle.
Chestnut had been rescued while swimming in the Atlantic
    Ocean.
She was captured after being hit by a fast moving motor boat.
Under intense observation, it was discovered she could
    mostly only float.
Chestnut stole my heart, injured but still working hard to
    paddle
Around by herself in a tank, looking so crooked as she
    sailed slowly by
Amazed by her deformed looking body and shell
I felt a genuine sadness as I gazed directly into her eye.
Unbelievable to see how she adapted to this unfortunate
    circumstance
Observers like me, fell in love with Chestnut at first glance.

I needed to learn more about these beautiful hard-shelled
    creatures.
Green turtles, like Chestnut, grow to be quite large with

many unique features.
Adults of this species commonly reach 100 cm in dorsal
   length and 150 kg in mass
Their underside is called a plastron and colors range from
   olive to black, so alas
I was getting to know more about Chestnut and how she
   came to be
Classified as an endangered species throughout the world's
   subtropical seas.
Because of her accident, Chestnut will probably never grow
   to full size
Now she remains in a tank all alone in the rescue center
   much to her surprise.
If she does grow larger she could move into a larger tank
   along with the sharks
Sea turtles can be mean, prefer to be alone, so is this a good
   life for her to start?

Chestnut made the best of a difficult situation, she didn't
   try to hide
She adapted, didn't give up, seemed rather content,
   paddling tilted on one side
She learned to swim back and forth in her limited and
   constricted space
It's testimony to God who cares for all his creations with an
   eternal grace.
I felt a sense of awe to witness the love and care given to
   this one injured turtle
Humans seem to complain about each little ache or pain as
   if its a major hurdle.

God watches over all the earth's creatures both great and small
So always give thanks for all your blessings
If you live without fear, pray for peace in this world, you
   will not fall
Find comfort in knowing God loves and protects us all.

Chapter 3:

Friends & Family

Barbara Welsh

Lessons from a Lime Tree

Hudson is the name of our lime tree.
If you read this poem you'll get to see
How this tree's name came to be.
An unusual name for a tree I agree.

We planted a lime tree in our backyard.
Our grandson Hudson was watching guard
Waiting for a lime to grow right before his eyes.
This didn't happen much to his surprise.

One by one he thought they would appear
We tried to explain but to him it wasn't clear.
If you say it is a lime tree where are the limes
They should be ready to pick all of the time.

We tried to explain it takes awhile for a lime to grow
But he was only five and how was he to know?
Whenever we look outside at that little lime tree
We think of Hudson and how uncomplicated life can be.

He is Interested in and curious about simple things,
Hopeful and excited for what each day brings.
Hudson, like a lime tree, requires tender loving care,
A place of safety and the focus of our prayers.

So there are many lessons to learn from a lime tree
And a grandson named Hudson that we did not foresee.
Life should be full of enthusiasm and optimistic feelings
That lead to new possibilities and purposeful meanings.

The Forever Friend

Come inside my tender heart
To slowly enter and become a part.
For you, it is a welcoming home
Settle down and make it all your own.

When two hearts are willing to risk it all,
Even if recently broken from a fall,
They will find a way to let it show.
That's the love I have come to know—
Love without any conditions,
Never afraid of competition.
Hope will break through like a knife
Even when shadows come upon my life.

I heard a gentle voice in my dreams,
Distinctly calling my name it seems
Like a gravitational pull.
My heart felt completely full.
So I'll push through the tiredness of my mind
Knowing we are somehow intertwined;
Once and for all time—
The forever friend of mine.

Happy Birthday to Quinn

Our youngest granddaughter is Quinn.
She is adorable with her sweet precious grin.
Quinn is a delightful remarkable little girl
Shiny and bright like a perfect and natural pearl.
She is uniquely talented with the purity of a child
Looking so innocent but sometimes can be a little wild.
For instance, picadillo is her favorite food
Not typical of what a 5-year old would usually include.
Her favorite color is blue and she loves to color and paint
And when it comes to unicorns you won't hear any
    complaint.
She loves all the "my little ponies" especially Rainbow
    Dash.
When she visits she gets into our hot tub and makes a big
    splash.
She's growing up so quickly and will start kindergarten
    next year.
Her 5th birthday is in June and we want to make it clear
That we wish her a happy birthday wrapped with lots of
    good cheer.
Praying God will keep her happy and safe as He protects
    from above
Because Quinn's birthday represents our family's circle of
    love.

Happy Birthday to Evelyn

Evelyn is celebrating her birthday.
She's our adorable granddaughter we're proud to say.
Her birthday is on July 28th when she will be six.
She is very busy and enjoys cheerleading and gymnastics.
She loves wearing Crocs, her preferred type of shoe
And her favorite color is a special shade of blue.
She decorates her Crocs with unicorn shoe charms
And likes to make bracelets for everyone's arm.
There are no in-betweens when it come to her actions
When she smiles and laughs it shows her satisfaction.
But when she frowns you have no doubt that she's mad
Especially if she's being scolded for fighting and being bad.
She likes to go to Target with her Mom and Dad to shop
And enjoys having play dates that continue until she drops.
Sometimes what she likes to do seems contradictory.
For instance, she likes to play Roblox and score a victory
And also loves playing in her room with her Barbies
Or going to birthday parties.
She loves swimming and Squishmallows stuffed animals
She is very smart and cute and her personality is
    magnanimous.
She's growing up so quickly so we want to make it clear
That we wish her a happy birthday wrapped with lots of
    good cheer.
We know her guardian angels are protecting her from above
Because Evelyn is a part of our family's circle of love.

Always and Forever a Mother

Once you become a mother,
A love blossoms inside unlike any other.
From the very first time a mother hears her baby's heartbeat
Her own heart swells with joy and nothing has ever felt so
  sweet.
Once a mother, a protective nature arrives and never
  disappears.
It grows and changes facing many challenges throughout
  the years.
A baby is a mother's sacred gift created for an existential
  reason.
Together they will travel through many different seasons.
Even when a mother's child grows into a young adult,
Her nurturing love continues to be the overpowering result.
Eventually when that child starts a family of his or her own
An inherent compassionate aptitude continues to be
  shown.
Grandchildren become a new dimension to a mother's life.
Her heart overflows with delight as this new facet takes
  flight.
Instinctively innocent they become the focus of her prayer
That life will be kind and the bond will always be there—
To serve eternally as an ever-present guardian angel,
With God as their protector from life's inevitable danger.

My Dads

I'm so glad I had a Dad
Who was kind, gentle and very sweet
My Dad always made me feel complete.
He kept me safe with unconditional love
Even when I may have acted like a clown.
He was my role model that's for sure
How could I have asked for anything more.
I miss him with all my heart
I was too young for us to part.

My grandfather was also special to me
I vividly remember him to this very day.
My sister and I loved to visit him and travel away
We would go to the beach and stay the whole day.
He was tall, very handsome and had a great wit
I miss him too and not just a little bit.

I'm lucky today to have two sons and a son in law
Now they are dads who always seem to give their all.
I'm proud of how each supports his own family
They exemplify what a father needs to be.

I will always have my heavenly Father as my guide
A Dad who loves me even when I may hide.
He sacrificed his only Son so that I am forgiven
Free to spend eternity with Him in heaven.

A Clock Named Joanne

Joanne doesn't go tic toc
She's an unusual type of clock
She plays beautiful tunes on the hour
Has moving parts like a super power
She only performs when it's light outside
Stays quiet in the dark like she's trying to hide
Serving as our alarm clock in the morning
Like a beautiful soloist always performing
Acquired from Joanne, my very good college friend
Becoming part of our home as a perfect blend
So we named the clock Joanne
Very odd some may say
To name a clock that way
A reminder that lasting friendship is a gift
Like sweet melodies too good to be missed.

Chapter 4:

Sell Yourself a Smile

Sell Yourself a Smile

Mother Teresa once said "peace begins with a smile."
A smile has the potential to light up someone's day
It is the universal language of kindness in many ways.
Smiling and saying hi to a stranger could change a life
Refresh and uplift spirits and take away daily strife.
The beauty of the soul is seen through a dazzling smile
It reflects a caring heart that can be felt for over a mile.
A smile is more important than the most stylist outfit you
    can wear
It is a sudden beam of sunlight like a hologram in the air.
Paint a few smiley faces on the walls of someone's heart
Illuminating the darkest corners with the light it imparts.
If you see someone without a smile why not give them
    yours
A smiling face is contagious, it will transfer and insure
That a promise is rendered as a motivation for grinning
When we believe there is a God who is loving and forgiving
Hopes and dreams tend to last a lifetime through
And possibilities are as endless as the sky is blue.
So sell yourself a smile and melt your defenses
Then give it away to help mend broken fences.

Say Goodbye, Say Hello

Say goodbye to a broken heart and a walking heartache
Say hello to a strong responsive heart that is awaken.
Say goodbye to past mistakes and regrets
Say hello to ways that help you to forget.
Say goodbye to blame and shame
Say hello to a new you who's not the same.

Untie the rope that binds
Leave the past behind
Then say goodbye to those chains and blinders
And say hello to a freer life that is much kinder.

Look the enemy in the eye
And say goodbye to all his lies.
Say hello to a new hope and purer love
And to your guardian angel from above.
Say goodbye to past sorrows and the resultant pain
Say hello to being born again and all you're set to gain.

Say goodbye to any bitterness and doubt that's ineffective
Say hello to positive energy and a new perspective.
Say goodbye to a fallen world with all its strife
Say hello to better attitudes and a divine new life.
Say goodbye to penalties and condemnation
Say hello to God's plan for a powerful new situation.
This is a plan for all that's good without fear of disaster
Providing a future of faith, joy and contentment now and
   ever after.

That Favorite Top

What to wear, what to wear?
Does anyone but you really care?
My closet has so many items
To pick from that's for sure/
Why do I automatically reach for…
That favorite top
That's never a flop
Makes my eye color pop
Someone said you look so thin
And it doesn't show too much skin
Besides it is my favorite color of blue!
I can't find another one so true
Maybe in a different color will do
Searching high and low
Almost broke my toe
Moving way too slow
Looking all over for a sale
Will I have to bail?
Or else go to jail!
Trying to find that top
Guess it's time to stop
Feeling like a flop
Because I love that favorite top!

COMICS
POW
BAM
KAPOW
WHAM
Yikes that is a big cat

See You in the Funny Papers

See you in the funny papers is a light-hearted way to say
  goodbye.
At least it was in the 1920's especially if you were quite shy.
Instead of saying see ya later it was a fun breezy way
To say hope you have a wonderful day.

Life is often very silly, funny, ironic like in a comic strip
But since it's not reality no one can give you any lip.
It's a cute and savvy phrase to say to a casual acquaintance
A sequence of notes sounding like a sweet melodic cadence.

While reading the daily comics you may be able to relate
To Lucy and Charlie Brown when on their first date.
Your cat may act like Garfield and is always asleep
Or your dog looks like Marmaduke and lies in a big heap.
Your grandson drives you crazy like Dennis the Menace
So much that you wish you could fly away to Venice.
Hagar the Horrible could be your brother
He calls every day to say he's in trouble.
Members of your family could star in Family Circus
Situations seem futile and don't serve any purpose.
You turn on the TV hoping to watch a war movie
The star acts like Beetle Bailey, not very groovy.
You look in the mirror and who do you see
Oh no, is it Blondie looking back at me?
So when you are reading today's Funny Papers
Look carefully and you may see yourself and get a laugh
Appearing as the butcher, the baker or the candlestick
  maker.

So to all my friends all I will say to you
See YOU in the Funny Papers; tootle loo.

Sense of Humor and Positivity

Smiling and laughing at something funny
Like a joke about a 10-foot tall bunny
Can change your mood from bad to good.
Positivity tops negativity, happy thoughts restored.

Having a sense of humor is good for your health
Improving overall quality of life and a feeling of wealth.
An essential life skill to help guard against depression
Eliminating anxiety and a tendency for aggression.

Lightheartedness, laughter, even silliness fills your life
    with gratitude
Seeing the worst in everything and everyone will lead to a
    bad attitude.
Today, there seems to be so many mad and angry people all
    around
Not listening and close-mindedness causes so much
    criticism to abound.

Mark Twain once said "Humor is a great thing." Not to be
    easily erased.
"Irritations and resentments fly away and a sunny spirit
    takes their place."
It is crucial for leaders to use humor and common sense.

Why do we think they have to be so formal and often
    tense?

People are more relate-able when they can laugh at their
    own life.
Compatibility and positivity are skills that eliminate
    unnecessary strife.
Blow off psychological steam with an activity or passion
    you enjoy.
Disconnecting from negative people can provide
    unexpected joy.

Lighten up, smile, be nonjudgmental and confident in what
    you believe
Be thankful not bitter, focus on making a difference, a goal
    worthy to achieve.
People with a sense of humor tend to be kind, thoughtful
    and peaceful.
Their hearts are pure, for they look to God and see that He
    is merciful.

Opal and Earl Pickles

Pickles is a very relate-able comic strip
Focusing on a retired couple who can be quite a trip.
Both in their 70's; their names are Earl and Opal Pickles.
At times, and that is most times, they act a little fickle.
It's fun to read about their efforts to enjoy retirement
That often turns out to be imperfect at best
Maintaining a harmonious relationship is always a daily
    test.
Earl Pickles wears suspenders, is bald, and his bushy
mustache is white.
He wears glasses hoping to improve his declining eyesight.
Opal Pickles usually is seen in a purple polka-dotted dress
Along with white sneakers and sometimes her hair is a
    mess.
Her pet cat Muffin loves to sit on her lap
As they both fall asleep and take an afternoon nap.
Roscoe is the name of their beloved and funny acting dog.
He has floppy ears and sometimes looks like he's in a fog.

Nelson Wolff is their grandson who is their pride and joy.
Having him visit is one thing in common they both do
    enjoy.
Sylvia is their daughter and her husband is Dan
They are Nelson's parents who often lend a hand.
Clyde, Earl's friend, and Pearl, Opal's sister, often disagree.
Everyday relate-able situations are hilarious as you will
    see.
If you read it daily, you'll soon become fond of all the
    Pickles
Laughing along so you can't stop the onslaught of
    uncontrollable giggles.
As Earl often says, "How come I always get blamed for the
    things I do?"
"Sure, I'll blame it on the dog it's time for him to get his
    due."
Like all of us, Earl and Opal often just throw up their hands
    and say
Let's both get pickled and today is as good as any other day.

Chapter 5:

Choose to Snooze

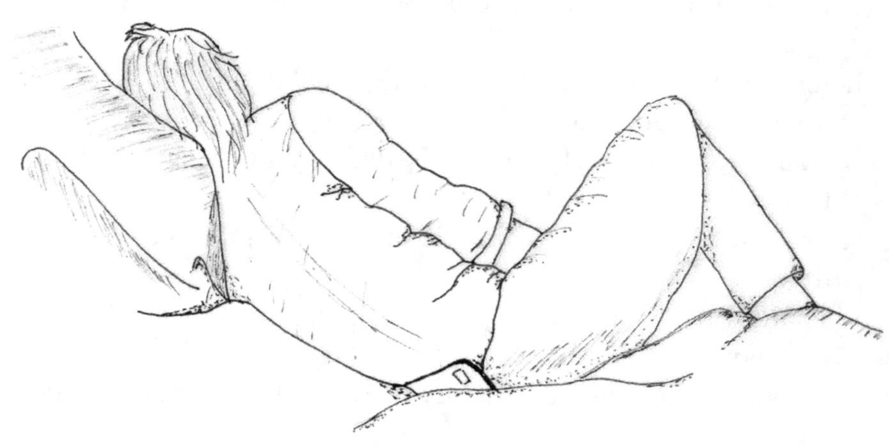

The Face of Forever

Where can you find the face of forever,
Does it come from a conscientious endeavor?
Is it an undertaking that takes boldness,
Extra strength without the coldness?
When faced with a critical and dire situation,
You need clear thinking to make the right decision,
Finding the fortitude to move forward,
Stepping calmly out and patiently onward,
Listening for a voice telling you what to do,
And looking for a road map to come into view.
Then holding the vision up to the light
As the face of forever comes into sight.
Your prayers are answered once again
As you close your eyes and count to ten.
You find the strength you never knew you had
Even if you don't understand why, just be glad
That His plan is amazing and everlasting;
Woven into the face of forever:
Always persistent and eternally withstanding.

Choose to Snooze

The saying "If you snooze, you lose"
Should be changed to say "choose to snooze".
If you value your sanity, composure and sense of mind
Or the tendency to remain calm and be kind
This may be the best information you'll find.

Not too long ago Facebook was created by some brilliant
    minds.
It was quite unique and one of the first of its kind.
It began as a way to locate old friends, it was very benign
A new way to communicate with old friends who decided
    to join
And find out more about them by viewing their stories
    online.

Fast forward to today and see how the focus has changed.
All the cute photos of families have been interchanged
Replaced with opinions you wish you could erase
Responses and comments you hope to replace.

I think I have found the perfect antidote
To avoid things you would never want to quote.
It's a new setting you can choose called snooze
Created so you really can't lose.

Your choices to select were either unfriend or block
You could always change the setting, it wasn't a lock.
Just all those offensive posts were locked and sent away
The problem was many people became offended that day
Whenever they saw you, they would look the other way.

Now you can just choose to snooze
Its only for 30 days so what do you have to lose.
This setting can make you happier and not as depressed
Negative comments you avoid and are no longer expressed.
Offensive remarks suddenly are toast
Gone by the snooze just like a ghost.

Throw It to the Wind

Words that hurt you
Words that hurt others too
Words of regret and bitterness
Words that spew negativity and distress
Words that weigh heavily on the mind—
Throw them into the wind to unwind
Whirling around and swiftly tossed
To fly away forever lost.

Learn to make wise decisions that will last
To outweigh mistakes made in the past.
Let them be swept away from your mind
Like hurtful speech that is unkind.

The tongue is a powerful weapon in disguise
Attempting to hold back the tongue is wise.
Prejudice will have no effect
If you treat everyone with respect.

Uncover untruths and faulty advice
So not to be forced to pay the price
For believing in unreliable resources.
Learn to control these harmful forces.

A limited perspective lacks wisdom
That can cause an unnecessary schism.
Look for expressions with authenticity
Don't be fooled by too much publicity.

Replace the world's advice with spiritual truth
Where purity of thought is not in dispute.
Release the pain of the past and let it float away
You are forgiven so carry on to live another day.

Barbara Welsh

Shout It From the Rooftops

If you want to share some good news publicly,
Something that really happened not hypothetically,
Shout it loudly far and wide from the rooftops
And soon you should receive a positive response.
Hearts and flowers arrive when you're expecting a new
    baby;
But perhaps not when you reveal that you just turned
    eighty.
Good and bad news spreads quickly from person to person
The meaning may be slightly altered with each dispersion.

Soon we will be celebrating some magnificent news.
If you step out of the darkness you'll find the clues.
They will be found in the morning light
When the good news comes into sight.
Be ready to shout it from the top of every mountain
As the water of life rises and flows up like a fountain.
The glory of the Lord will be revealed
Victorious in death so the earth will be healed.
Spread the word that He has risen;
Freed from the chains of a worldly prison.
Our sins are forgiven and wiped away
Because Jesus, the Over-comer, is here to stay.
The true meaning of Easter is unveiled
Goodness and mercy has prevailed.
We can shout it from the rooftops each and every day
Because the greatest success story has been displayed.

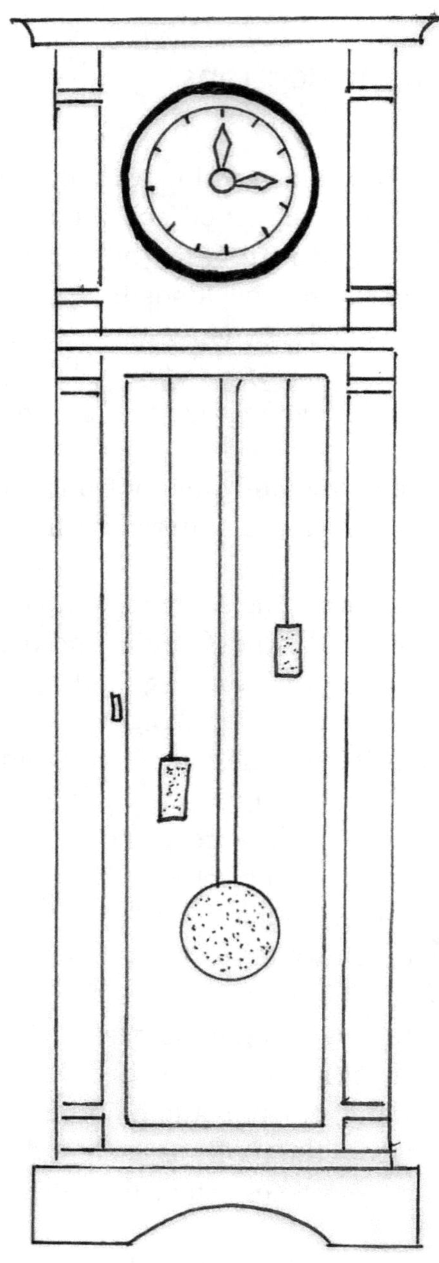

As a Pendulum Swings

A pendulum with its razor-sharp edge is one of the symbols
of time
Similar to a clock except when the minute hand hits 12, it
may chime.
A pendulum's position is said to oscillate back and forth
Regulating the movement of clocks and metronomes at
their source.
The pendulum swings and vacillates under the influence of
gravity
Its movement is suspended from a fixed position of neutrality.
Life is a like a pendulum that swings between joy and tears
Sense and nonsense, love and hate, courage and fears.
But can it measure the difference between right or wrong
Maintaining a balance of morality for who knows how long?
Opinion is like a pendulum that obeys the same rule
There are two sides to every story, each with a notion as its
fuel
Allowing freedom of expression without censorship or
intolerance
For understanding to prevail, it's essential to eliminate one-
sided dominance.
Our culture is set up to rely on a series of checks and balances
Because history reflects many pendulum swings and
challenges.
Theoretically, a pendulum will oscillate forever when there
is no friction
Similarly, true love endures for a lifetime with a limited
number of conflicts and contradictions.

Chapter 6:

A Shoulder to Cry On

Barbara Welsh

A Shoulder to Cry On

You can cry on my shoulder
I am here as your beholder.
A true friend is a genuine treasure.
Their worth is impossible to measure.
A friend exhibits mutual trust
Especially when you need to readjust.
Consistently close to your heart
Seldom happy when apart
Sympathetic during good or bad occasions
Helping you to solve life's difficult equations
Lending a shoulder to cry on when needed
Saying a prayer to be spoken or pleaded
Like the power of a special dance or song
A memory that lasts for oh so long
A friend makes you smile and laugh more.
Never finds fault or keeps score
Is there to catch you when you fall
Your sounding board if you should call
So my friend, you can cry on my shoulder.
Now and forever as we grow older
Anytime, anywhere
Tears of love we share
Eternal hearts to care.

To The-Moon-and-Back Kind of Love

If you tell someone you love them to the moon and back
Will it help to keep your relationship on the right track?
Is it a romantic way to express your feelings
That may have a strong and everlasting meaning?
At 250,000 miles away, don't expect to get there soon.
It will take three days to travel one way to the moon.
Is saying you love someone to the sun and back a better
story
Or just another expression to add to your inventory?
It is 93 million miles away and takes 223 days—
Now maybe this will set your love-life ablaze!
Perhaps you've tried saying I love you to infinity and
beyond.
Maybe this sentiment will come across as more profound.
Infinity is endless and therefore cannot be reached;
Consequently limitless possibilities have now just
increased.
Have you ever heard anyone say I love you to the planet
Saturn?
This phrase could be the most useful and melodramatic
pattern.
Because to travel to Saturn it takes about seven years;
Therefore Saturn would logically outweigh all others it
appears.
So which is the most romantic way to say I love you?
Perchance saying words more sincere and simple will do.
Manifesting a beautiful feeling that comes from your heart
With a promise to love and cherish and never to part.

Now

Say I love you now and again tomorrow
Feel the joy today to avoid regret and sorrow.
There are no guarantees for a second chance
To sense the love, adoration and romance.
If you have found the love of your life hold them tight
You never know if it's the last time you'll kiss good night.
Love is like a fly on the wall you have to catch it while you
    can
Hold on tightly, savor moments, focus on a new plan
One that doesn't put off time together to another day
This could be the final season so why should you delay.
Time is fleeting so try not to wait or hesitate
Or decide to postpone that special trip to a later date.
The stream you are floating down is beyond your control
You can't stop and rewind you're caught up in its flow.
Listen to the words to a popular song, *'Til you can't...*
Don't wait on tomorrow 'cause tomorrow may not show
Say your sorries, your I-love-yous, 'cause man you never
    know.

In the Moment

Keep me in the moment
It's where my life needs to be
My future is yet to see.

Yesterday is gone and can't be changed.
Tomorrow is a mystery to be rearranged.
This moment in time is all we are assured
With eyes wide open to see what's in store.
We can't change anything that happened in the past.
Stop, slow down, be thankful for the things that last.
Look at a flower or bird, enjoy its beauty right now.
Tomorrow it may be gone; not yours to wonder how.
Each moment's presence is a present.
Make it fruitful, worthwhile and pleasant.
Faith and joy are visible in a million different ways.
When the sun rises or sets we see its powerful rays.
Cherish life's experiences provided for us today.
Tomorrow will bring with it different surprises.
Be patient, have faith, and wait for new horizons
Worrying about what lies ahead will not change a thing.
God is in control, have faith in what He will bring.
Focus on what you can control.
Otherwise frustration may take its toll.

Everywhere I Go

Everywhere I go You're not far away
Today, tomorrow and yesterday.
Many times I feel alone
But I'm never really on my own.

When my world comes crashing in
You whisper to me like a mellow violin.
You're next to me the entire time.
That is my life's unique design.

You answer my prayers if You see fit
So I never get to the point of having to quit.
If I don't doubt, but believe and remain strong
With patience nothing can go wrong.

Life is not easy, many things seem unfair.
We each have a relatable story to share.
Words of understanding can help someone in need
When we carefully listen and then proceed.

God expects us to help each other and be kind
We're part of the big picture with our lives intertwined.
If we coexist with tolerance to show we understand
He will be with us everywhere we go holding our hands.

Stars

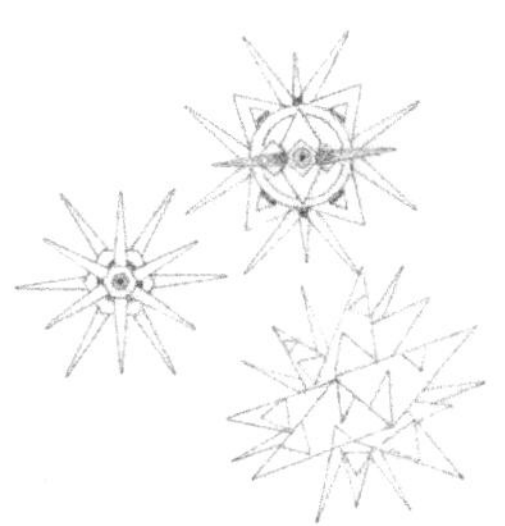

God placed the stars in the sky,
For us to question and wonder why.
He knows each star by name,
Although they appear much the same.

Stars are born within clouds of dust,
From our vantage point they look powerful and robust.
They shine so brightly against the vast dark sky above—
These astronomical objects are designed with love.

We see stars that are not only celestial;
In life's star-studded journey they are essential.
To serve daily as earthly symbols everywhere,
Glittery stars are woven into fabrics we wear.

The American flag is referred to as the Star-Spangled Banner;
When unfurled, fifty stars are displayed in a glorious manner.
Like a star-studded cast in a motion picture or play
That mesmerizes the onlooker in several ways.

The Star of Bethlehem served as a light to follow from afar.
It is a bright and beautiful five-pointed Yuletide star
That plays a huge part in the story of the Nativity,
Celebrated at Christmas as an annual day of festivity.
To some, Jesus is the most significant star ever born,
Bringing peace and joy to the hopeless and forlorn.

Our hearts and minds become stars of reflection
To showcase God's love and shield of protection.
We can be an efficacious star if we choose to be—
A guiding light to the future for all the world to see.

Chapter 7:

Would the Real Pinocchio Please Stand Up?

Would the Real Pinocchio Please Stand Up?

Liar, liar pants on fire!
How soon will your nose start to grow?
Is Pinocchio in the building? How are we to know?
Unconfirmed reports coming from anonymous sources
Without checking facts or any reliable resources.
Just make it up and see if it sticks.
You know how to use all of your tricks.
Many readers and viewers are somehow blindly led.
They believe everything they see; so easily misled.
There's no honor or reliability in journalism today.
Emotions are manipulated to make you think only one way.
Information reported may not be based on fact
Causing confusion to steer us way off track.
Pinocchio is a fictional character of course
Notably characterized by a frequent tendency to lie with no
    remorse.
Causing his nose to grow longer and longer.
Getting away with it only makes him stronger.
So would the real Pinocchio please stand up?
We need to be told the truth not trust it just to luck.
Or have to search for long noses and still be stuck.
A Pinocchio won't look you straight in the eye.
They will just look away and say man whassup!

Eliminating the Fear Factor

When you listen to the news do you feel distraught?
Do they think you'll forget all that you've been taught;
Trying to make you afraid of something that is unreasonable
To intensify Covid-19's fear factor until you believe it is
    feasible?
Politicians and the media use fear to make us hate without
    thinking;
The surprising thing is educated people fall for it and start
    overthinking.
Even normally intelligent people become brainwashed by it.
Fear is a thief that steals truth-based thinking and logic.
Life is full of faith stealers like doubt, stress and uncertainty
But fear can be the most harmful because it causes more
    anxiety.
Fear is a human response to situations we don't understand,
Over which we have no control so they remain in command.
So this becomes our reality as we peer into the future;
Intensifying, crippling and growing like a malignant tumor
As part of the enemy's arsenal to wreak havoc through fear;
Diminishing our faith hoping our belief in God will disappear.
It is hard not to submit to it and focus only on the negative;
Fight the fear, stand strong, and allow God to control your
    narrative.

The Vindictive Poltergeists

Do you know anyone who has a desire for revenge
With a troublesome grudge they hope to avenge?
They may have some wild and wacky tendencies
Including disturbing and gruesome-type dependencies.
Poltergeists are a type of ghost or noisy spirit
Screeching so loud that you try not to hear it.
They exhibit strange movements and are capable of levitation
Looking like predators or some type of non-human
   aberration.
If lights begin flickering and objects fly through the air
And all of a sudden a fire starts in your hair
You should immediately hide and take cover
Because they can soar like a flash and sometimes hover.
They are known for harassing and tormenting their victims
Right out of a horror story using little or no wisdom.
Vindictive poltergeists are the worst kind to encounter
You could even become an ingredient in their next pot of
   chowder.
They may attempt to hit you, bite, pinch or trip
In defense you might want to carry a lasso or whip
Always be prepared and ready for battle
Put on your armor and carry a paddle.
They walk amongst us every day
Will destroy you if you get in their way
Or they don't agree or like what you say.

Tacky Tourists

Here come the tacky tourists
Can we send them to Honduras?
Wearing bright silly looking hats,
And they always want to stop and chat.
Bright turquoise sunglasses cover their eyes,
Maybe they want to stay in disguise.
Often wearing thin white socks, one high, one low
Lost, they ask for directions and drive real slow.
Binoculars are dangling around their necks.
Purple sandals with socks, did they think to check?
Wearing a bathing suit in the grocery store,
Kids with flamingo floaties worn while they explore.
Taking selfies left and right,
Staying out late every night,
Causing traffic jams and long waiting lines—
So maybe we should make them pay a few fines.
In the winter, Florida is a popular tourist spot
Yet they all skedaddle when it starts to get hot.

Idle Talk

Gossip, hasty words and idle talk
Will cause any listener to want to balk.
They hear words sounding like gibberish
Unintelligent, nonsensical and childish.

Consider what to say before you respond
So the message relayed is more profound.
Make each word you say count
To avoid hesitation or any doubt.

Try to cultivate a measured reply
Not idle words that don't apply.
A gentle answer turns away wrath
Harsh words lead down the wrong path.

Useless words create misunderstanding
Precise and clear speech is more outstanding.
It tends to bring to light positive thoughts
More effective in getting a point across.

Never belittle, tease, laugh at or mock
It intimidates and results in unnecessary shock
That will often cause hurt feelings to arise
Saying nothing at all can be incredibly wise.

Take all hurtful words and thoughts to the wind
To be blown away to let all the good ones begin.

ANOTHER
BIRTHDAY

Barbara Welsh

Another Birthday

Another year older I fear
Why can't I skip this year?
Each birthday rolls around too fast;
As a kid it was such a blast.
I think I have a Birthday phobia
It is really a fear called *fragapanophobia*.

Birthdays remind us we're getting older.
Don't carry the birthday blues on your shoulder.
Nobody is counting or will make the correction.
Why not start counting in the opposite direction?
If you are celebrating a milestone or tangible marker in
    time,
Have fun, be silly; you're not committing a crime.

Think young and stay active by enjoying every day
Always acting positive by pushing the negative away.
When the impossible becomes possible
And there's so much more to achieve...
Nothing is out of reach when you choose to believe.
Do what you like, then you'll like whatever you do
Or even try something new and exciting for you.

In your mind you're still the same person
You were when you were twenty-one —
A perpetual teenagers always having fun.
Avoiding mirrors keeps you feeling forever young
"I'm way too young to be this old," you say
Triggering happy memories to chase the blues away.

Chapter 8:

Healing a Broken Heart

Healing a Broken Heart

Love is a lesson that isn't taught in school
You don't learn it from a book as a general rule.
Hearts are broken when you lose someone
As the score in the game of life is lost or won.
Whether it's your choice or not to say goodbye
You try to hide your tears when you want to cry.
How do you hide a broken heart
Do you hear a sound when it breaks apart?
You can chase a new dream when it's right for you
By focusing on what's positive to shine a light on what to do.
If you call or visit a friend who has a more pressing need
It takes your mind off yourself saying it's time to proceed.
God provides a road map when you seek direction on your
    path
By loving, living and letting go of bitterness and wrath.
The tiniest bit of hope that dwells in a heart that is broken
Will mend with kind words spoken and thoughts unspoken.

Amazing and All Powerful

If the world feels like a lonely place
Because you are tired of the rat race
And scared of growing old
From all that you've been told.
You don't know where time has gone
You often feel somewhat withdrawn.
People sometimes seem unkind
And a non-judgmental friend is hard to find.
It might appear like there's no hope
If you feel strung out and at the end of your rope.
What once was wrong is now considered right
The country is falling apart, everyone is so uptight.
You read negative sentiments on a coffee cup
Often feel so tired that you can't keep up.
Do you need a break today
But regrets seem to get in the way?
Find comfort knowing God walks in your shoes
You can change it all with His good news.
He is amazing and all powerful
So turn to Him and remain prayerful.
He put the stars in the sky
You do not need to ask Him why.
He causes the sun to shine
It's part of His unique design
Indescribable and unchangeable
Always true, non-comparable
Never wavering, always the same
Miraculous and marvelous to proclaim.
He will never let you down.
He is trustworthy and profound.
You no longer have to live each day on your own
And never again feel isolated and all alone.

What Good Is It?

What good is a checklist if you never check it
Not very useful you have to admit.
What good is a prayer if it is never prayed
Without prayer you may always be afraid.
What good is a thought if it is never expressed
It fades from memory and will never be assessed.
What good is a grocery list if you leave it at home
Up and down all the aisles you will have to roam.
What good is a phone call if it is never made
Like a song on the radio that is never played.
What good is a card if it is never sent
No one will know your true intent.
What good is a project that you never complete
You will gradually feel a sense of defeat.
What good is a book if it is never read
It just sits on the shelf or beside your bed.
What good is a promise that you do not keep
People may not trust you the next time you speak.
What good is love if you don't give it away
You may not have the chance on another day.

The Torn Veil

When Jesus died, the temple veil was torn from top to
  bottom.
This action foresaw that something very special would
  blossom.
An earthquake occurred exactly at the time of Jesus's death.
If the quake had ripped the veil as Jesus took his last breath
It would have been torn from the bottom upward.
But as the earth separated and His final words were heard
The invisible hands of God reached down
Removing the barrier that had kept Him bound.
He tore the veil in order to ensure personal accessibility
And to forgive us for our worldly instability.
Jesus paid the ultimate price for our iniquities and sins
With repentance, the promise of eternal life begins.
If you commit, you will be held securely in God's hands
The anxieties and stressors you face will no longer
  withstand.
Let go of the problems you try to conquer on your own
Turn them over to God so you don't face them all alone.
The torn veil represents the advocate available to you every
  day.
He is there by your side ready to guide and direct your way.

I Run to You

I run to You when I am weary
Trying to focus when I am teary.
If life throws me a curve ball
I try to face it head on so I won't fall.
When worry collects and fills my mind
I fight the thoughts that make me blind
So I can visualize what is right in front of me.
I need to concentrate so I will clearly see
Your face with its comforting smile
To refresh and renew me for awhile.
When my foundation has been shaken
You give me strength if I'm forsaken.
When I feel like no one listens
I run to You to help me re-position;
To take away the pain and erase my frown
So the weight of adulthood won't bring me down.
Walk beside me, hold me tight
I run to You because I know it's right.
A time will come when the future is clear
When rainbows and celestial stars appear.

Follow Truth

If you struggle with trusting
You may need some readjusting.
Skepticism and fear set in when faith steps out.
Without hope there will be struggles and doubt.
Faith is believing something without seeing,
A conviction that creates a feeling of well-being.
Refuse to let your doubts grow,
Resist with firmness and your strength will show.
Your heart will follow and reflect only the truth.
If you do what is right, there will be no excuse.
There is no need to have to impress anyone
When purity of heart shines forth like the sun.
If you follow truth it will quiet your soul
No explanation is needed or tale to be told—
Solid and steadfast, tranquil and calm,
Free from disturbance like a soothing balm.
The waves of completeness and harmony of mind
Extend to gifts of peace and forgiveness—yours to find.

Chapter 9:

On the Bumpy Road to Happiness

On the Bumpy Road to Happiness

Happiness is a direction, not a place
You have to take it slow, it's not a race.
It is a by-product, a secondary result
A sought-after feeling that you hope to exalt.
No medicine will cure what happiness can't
It's not in your power to bestow or grant.
There's always going to be bumps in the road
Along with stumbling blocks you can't avoid using a secret
    code.
It is wise to treat these obstacles as steppingstones
Finding ways to solve life's puzzle of unwelcome
    unknowns.
The road to happiness will have adversity, there are no
    guarantees
You hope for smooth sailing with good weather and soft
    summer breezes.
Your road may be fraught with barricades and uncharted
    terrain
As your character is tested, mistakes will be made with
    only you to blame.
Finding happiness is a test of strength and a form of courage
Hard to understand and easy to underestimate its
advantage.
Tears may poignantly fall from overwhelming grief you
    encounter
Reflecting love surrendered with an impact convincingly
    profounder.
Maybe happiness is not a destination but a path of all you
    leave along the way
With the simple acts of kindness you deliver and
    thoughtful words you say.

Looking for a Good Ending

Most people are good is what I hear others say
I pray this is true in most every way.
Most mothers and fathers are loving and kind
They would never leave their child behind.
It seems to happen more than we know
But on the surface it may never show.
Abuse is real in many situations causing harm
When too much hate and anger set off an alarm.
Doing what is right seems to be swept away with the tide
Evidenced when questionable behavior is taken in stride.
When something once wrong is now considered right
We lose control of values that used to be within sight.
Truth becomes altered and not recognizable anymore
Maybe that's why people close their eyes and simply ignore.
Repeating a line that may sound good but isn't based on
    fact
Allows lies to be accepted as truth without any negative
    impact.
When selfishness looms large pain lingers on
So peace is not available when needed to rest upon.
A hasty decision can haunt you for the rest of your life
As time goes on it festers and pierces like a knife.
What could have been remains a part of your thoughts
You can forgive yourself but forgetting is often naught.
If you know in your heart what is right
Truth will resonate and find the light.
When looking for a good, not perfect, ending
You find a supernatural love transcending.

One Less Day

When the sun goes down and I close my eyes
There will be one less day to enjoy a new sunrise
One less day to make a difference and change a heart
Forgive and make a resolution for a brand new start.

As the days go by I think of how much time I've wasted
There's so much more of life I could have tasted.
As I get older I feel I'm in a race against time
Trying to get in things I missed while in my prime.

Seeing the light pass through my windows
Feeling the salt and sand trickle between my toes,
I realize these simple pleasures have been taken for granted
So I wonder if enough love and kindness has been planted.

Dribbles of happy thoughts pass through my mind
Serving as a focal point of memories soft and kind.
Seeing my life through a rainbow-colored kaleidoscope
Produces thoughts of enlightenment and words of hope.

I don't want to stay on a train with a one-way track
Making more mistakes I can't take back.
I need to focus on the future not run around in circles
It's impossible to go back and retract; there are no reversals.

Every day there's one less day to read another story
Compose and write another poem of peaceful glory
Dance another dance, sing another song
And say I love you with tenderness and a hug to go along.

If we consider each new day as a privilege
We can begin to visualize a glorious heavenly image.
Then instead of thinking we have one less day
We'll start to see a much brighter day is not far away.

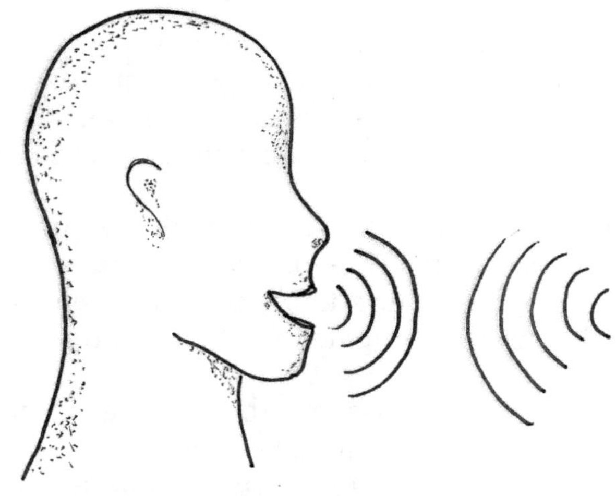

Echoes

Poetry creates an echo of thoughts and feelings
The repetition of sensations that a heart is revealing.
An echo is a noise caused by the reflection of sound waves
Resonating and rebounding like a signal or familiar phrase.

When you shout into a canyon you hear the echo of your
     voice
Like music that repeats notes that may cause you to rejoice.
Life serves as an echo because what you send out returns to
     you
You sow what you reap without time to intercept and review.

Be a voice not an echo that repeats baseless viewpoints you
     hear
Think for yourself, analyze, research, don't be taken
     hostage by fear.
If you exist in an echo chamber talking only to people in
     which you agree
Nothing is gained, it's a one-sided path with no reward or
     guarantee.

If you don't like being judged by others then do not judge
It will force you to carry around an unsubstantiated grudge.
Spewing out hatred allows bitterness to filter back through
But radiating and giving love results in love coming back to
     you.

Side Trip to a Side Trip

In life we start out on one single path
That often leads us to take a side trip to provide a good
    laugh.
Then each side trip takes its own side trip so with joy we
    do leap
Until we wonder is this our first side trip that at first
    seemed so steep.
Or is it another trip's side trip so we rinse and repeat.

It was a very pleasant road we were on
Until this unexpected side trip began.
It came without warning
We needed to face it as best as we can.

We were following a simple routine enjoying our friends
    and family.
We always knew at any one time where we needed to be.
We liked being in our comfort zone and nice little bubble
Not wavering or making too much trouble.

All of a sudden we were caught in a trap
Thrown a curve ball and we had to adapt.
Lost our direction and took an unexpected detour
Sort of like learning a new musical score.

The side trip took its own side trip.
We found new ways to be entertained
Adjusting so we wouldn't go insane.
We floundered around trying to make sense of it all
Like a new baby learning to crawl.

Perhaps we will discover a bright light at the end of the
    tunnel
We must follow the guidelines or be sifted out through a
    funnel
Never expecting we would have to wear a mask
And learn social distancing it's part of the task.
Why do we have to cancel all future travel
Isolate and stay at home, try not to unravel?

How many side trips to each side trip will we be asked to
    take
Before we wander on the wrong side trip and make a
    mistake.
Stay focused, don't question or ponder what is really at
    stake.

Why did this happen we ask, what is our final trip plan?
If you turn all your side trips over to God
He'll provide comfort and safety, if we allow Him He can.
Trust that God is in control and with Him we stand.

Chapter 10:

Silver Linings

A Silver-Linings Person

What do you normally say,
The glass is half empty or half full?
Do you like things obvious or more obscure?
Do you look for a silver lining, a sign of hope
Or are you always negative and at the end of your rope?
Are you a silver-linings person
Or do you think every situation is bound to worsen?
Do you look for the positive aspect
Or is it only the unfavorable one you expect?
"Every cloud has a silver lining" is a metaphor for optimism
Leaving little room for the dark clouds of pessimism.
How do you react when you realize a battle is in front of you?
Faced with hardship, do you let thoughts of defeat filter
    through.
So you're left feeling angry or exhausted can't focus on
    anything else,
Carrying the burden on your back, complaining about all
    the stress.
Satan rejoices, he enjoys making you feel everything is
    going wrong
Blaming God is a major victory, as he hopes to increase and
    prolong.
God helps you to see there's good all around.
He will point out all the advantages to be found
While converting you to a silver-linings person.
Trust is fragile like a flower.
Faith will make you strong and give you the power
To sift out, isolate and remove the negative.
Faith cushions the bumps in the road like a natural sedative
Or a silver lining sewn into the numerous clouds drifting above
As the sun weaves and shines through God's satiny fabric
    of Love.

Changing From the Inside Out

In certain types of ovens food cooks from the inside out.
Friction of molecules distributes heat throughout.
People also change starting on the inside.
Hearts and minds adapt as alterations are applied
Then reshaped on the outside to be shown to the world.
It's a process that takes time before noticed and observed.
Often we allow external influences to determine how we act.
Push them aside, trust your instincts and don't overreact.
As a transformation occurs, you realize you're not the same
    person.
Only in growth, reform and change; your true self makes its
    assertion.
Lean on God's promises and courage will be released from
    within.
The fear and doubt you inwardly felt subsides as your new
    story begins.
A renewed strength shines intrinsically when belief in God
    is responsible
For all that you do and say; what was once impossible
    becomes possible.

More to This Life

There's more to this life than just living and dying.
Don't waste time complaining and not even trying.
Learn to live life to the fullest each and every day
Instead of hoping you'll find a better way.
There's just one truth, one way, one story
One road to be on that reflects God's glory.
Set idealistic and lofty things aside
Clear a path for God to provide
Don't be a drifter without a home
You never have to feel alone.
Whatever may come, you're in good hands
With a gentle touch you'll be shown a plan.
Focus on the good, the pure, and the forgiven
The way will be revealed with clarity and precision.
If you're easily upended when uncertainty arises
Turn your burdens over to God, there will be no reprises.
He guides and provides comfort so you'll no longer be
  shaken
Providing a refuge and promise to never be forsaken.

Round-the-Clock Love

Voices in your mind say you're not enough
Struggles you feel everyday seem so rough
There's a battle raging in your mind
Until you hear a gentle whisper that's so kind.

Each day you have many highs and many lows.
Time often seems to pass along too slow.
Open your eyes so you can see.
Ask for shelter to set you free.

Trust and believe that you can conquer fear.
The comforting hand of God is always near
To calm worries that come in the dead of night.
The Lord will fight your battle, He knows what's right.
Weakness and doubt will be replaced with courage and
    strength.
Burdens will be lifted; His round-the-clock love will be
    dispensed.
God's love will justify your life and fill you with hope for
    what lies ahead
Giving you a new and fresh destination under God's
    direction instead.
Love that's unconditional and divine so that it cannot be
    severed.
Take comfort in knowing God truly loves you now and
    forever.

Two Choices

Many times in life there are only two choices
Before making a choice be sure to listen to trusted voices.
You can choose to have faith or to live in worry and fear
With doubt you can miss seeing the choice that is clear.
Either by searching out truth or falling for whatever is
    trending
It is your responsibility to make sure you are accurately
    comprehending.
Just because others say something is true, you still should
    question
What you hear even if it sounds acceptable and with good
    intentions.
Think for yourself and don't be fooled by mass deceit
That creates a domino effect so you are tempted to repeat.
Truth insists on faithfulness and trusts God's power to
    resist error
The enemy tempts us with words disguised as truth to
    elicit terror.
A person in tune with God will reject false teaching and
    listen for truth
Not be fooled or swayed but remain on watch like a warrior
    or sleuth.
Vulnerability clouds the truth so weakness instead of
    strength is unfurled
Choose to live with God in control, not alone, or what
    manipulates the world.

Chapter 11:

Pedicures & Pinky Toes

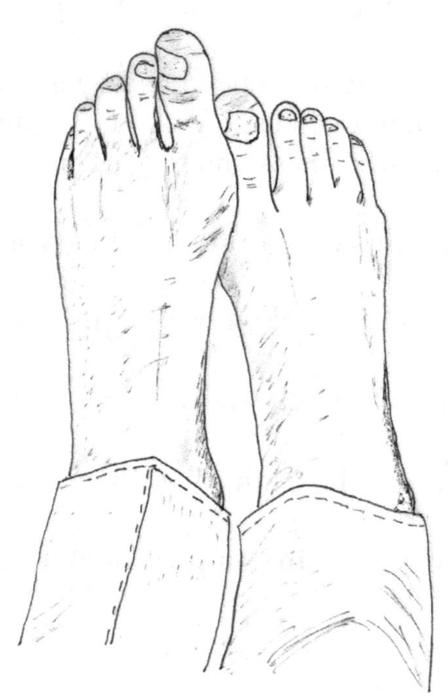

Pedicures and Pinky Toes

I used to think pedicures were only for the elite
Now they're like my favorite pampering treat.
It's nice to have a chance to sit, soak and relax,
Especially when your feet are tired and exercised to the max.
It's difficult to manicure and paint your pinky toes just right
And avoid getting polish all over creating an unwelcome sight.
Pinky toes are a part of our body we tend to forget
Until the minute one is hurt or broken and then we get upset.
Why do you think God added the pinky toe onto our feet?
To remind us when we stump it that it'll never be obsolete.
What does your nail tech call a man with a rubber toe?
The nail tech calls him Roberto.
Do you know any jokes about toes that are funny
To lighten your day and make it more sunny?
Okay, what has three feet but no toes?
It's a yardstick with no toes to show.
What did the man call the bee that had a toe?
He called him Toby, if you really want to know.
How do feet store their memories in life?
With pho-toes taken with their phone or other device.
Which toes make a great mouth freshener?
Men-toes because they are the perfect breath refresher.
All kidding aside, our feet and toes can serve as messengers.
They have the ability to carry forth personal blessings
Taking you far and wide for you to make a difference
By telling others about salvation and God's true magnificence.

Songs and Serenades

People sing songs to many different tunes
Some sing in the morning, others prefer the afternoon.
Everyone likes a melody that reflects love and
understanding
A harmony of notes that to the heart is so enchanting.
A serenade sung to you may be an unsuspected surprise
It sometimes triggers tears to start pouring from your eyes.
Perhaps it resonates the memory of a past love that was lost
Seeing the writing on the wall, you had to pay the cost.
You found the courage and strength to finally let it go
Even though your face tried not to let it show.
Your heart felt the sting until the healing could start
As it listened for sounds of tranquility to quietly impart.
Like the murmur of a bird singing a sweet refrain
Or the aura of the ocean to ease away the pain.
Songs and serenades provide a fresh point of view
To replenish and renew when sung to only you.
They enable you to pause, rest, and think before you begin
A new song about the changes that are coming from within.

Perfect Pairs

Some things in life seem to go together
Like salt and pepper or a bird and a feather.
There are people who tend to connect
Always producing a lasting effect.
Pairs like Bogie and Bacall and Bonnie and Clyde
Consistently seem to belong side by side.
Perfect pairs, couples, sisters and twins
Without each other appear lost and unable to win.
Many different foods make a perfect combination
They create a familiar mouth-watering sensation.
For example, macaroni and cheese tastes very yummy
While rice and beans or bacon and eggs fill your tummy.
There are cartoon-character pairs who are everyone's
    favorites.
Tom and Jerry and Mickey and Minnie have become major
    hits.
Best friends stick together through thick and thin.
Husband and wife, mothers and daughters feel love from
    within.
If you have a loving connection with God and He dwells in
    your heart
You've made a quintessential pair that undoubtedly sets
    you apart.

That New Car Smell

You buy a new car and can't help loving that smell of it
  being brand new.
So special and unique you listen when told it will last
  forever for you.
You want to believe that life will provide comfort like this
  one-of-a-kind smell.
However, that aromatic comfort pales in comparison to
  what you have yet to tell.
The new car smell is a metaphor for the birth of your first-
  born baby girl or boy
A new life experience; you never knew you could feel so
  much emotional joy.
You're overwhelmed as you realize the miracle you have
  recently witnessed.
Hoping the euphoria, like the new car smell, lasts so you
  feel forever blessed.
Fast forward to today, your new grandchild has arrived, it's
  a new baby boy
That new car smell is back and your heart once again is
  overflowing with joy.

Bumps and Lumps

Are you a bump on a log
Or would you rather be a frog
It's better than being a hog
And stand outside in the fog.

I used to be quiet
Till I went on a diet
Now I talk all the time
And make everything rhyme.

I love to see something red
When I first jump out of my bed
And try to clear my head
It wakes me up in a flash
Then I can quickly dash
To the kitchen to drink my coffee at last.

Life is a mystery
You have to look hard to see
What you really want it to be
Or be happy to just drink iced tea.

I like to eat salad
It's good for the palate
With vitamins galore
It's never a bore
Unless you make it a chore.

Root beer is very tasty
So don't be hasty
You'll thank me a bunch
When you drink it for lunch
Unless it makes you burp
Then you'll think I'm a jerk.

Chapter 12:

Stop! Think it Over.

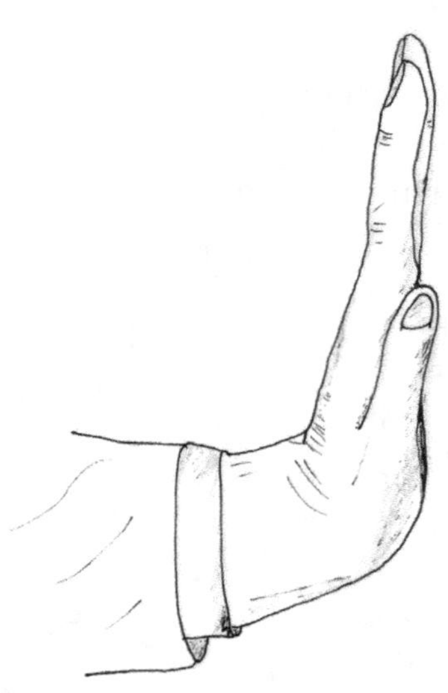

Stop! Think it Over.

Do the lyrics in a song by the Supremes come to mind
Asking you to think it over before saying words that are
    unkind?
Conversations can be like the sun as it shines through the rain
Or like dark clouds that block out the sun causing hurt and
    pain.
Lessons from the Bible give instructions to be quick to
    listen
And slow to speak in order to portray an agreeable
    disposition.
In today's information society we have shorter attention spans
Everyone wants to get and receive answers as fast as they can.
They don't want to be filibustered by a talkaholic
Until they cease to listen or have turned catatonic.
Some people keep talking about anything and everything
    and don't stop
Every time you say something they jump back in until your
    head wants to pop.
Most people have good intentions but speak using way too
    much detail
Then the listener makes an excuse to exit so their mind
    won't derail.
Others talk incessantly about themselves not allowing
    anyone else to speak
The conversation is all about them until the person
    listening starts to feel weak.
It takes focused discipline and willpower not to talk too much
So stop first to listen intently then respond with a loving
    touch.

A Witness in the Silence

Everything seems clearer
Because You are nearer.
Your presence is irresistible
As each day grows more predictable.

With every breath I take
I know You won't forsake.
Through valleys, rivers and into streams
You appear beside me in my dreams.

Everyone reaches out for peace
Looking for a way to find relief;
Mending and healing every heart
So pain and suffering will not be a part.

Help us to be a witness in the silence
To ease the noise from idle nonsense;
Giving hope by lending a helping hand
To form a solid foundation on which to stand.

Sharing a personal testimony forms a cascade
That often sets off a sequential crusade;
Causing a ripple effect to those who hear
As the message of salvation becomes clear.

Why Didn't I Call

I suspected something was wrong
I hadn't heard from you in way too long.
But time slipped away.
I said it could wait one more day.

Soon I would call to check and see
I lingered too long, what's wrong with me.
Was it destiny or fate
Or was I just too late!

Why didn't I call?
What a shame, that's all.
Never put it off, call her or him
Even if it is just on a whim.

Your voice might just be what is needed
Words of encouragement superseded.
Don't say you don't have time today
So you decide to delay another day.

Make an effort to let someone know you care.
You might eliminate unnecessary despair.
It is preferable to be reassured and glad
Than face regret, feel sad and wish you had.

I Love My Lanai

What's a lanai?
Many people will ask.
Especially people who live up north.
They always want to call it a porch
Or sometimes even a deck.
But I say what the heck!
Another name may be a patio.
Can it then be used as a studio?
It may also be called a veranda.
Do friends go there to meander?
You never heard of a lanai?
I just look at them and sigh.
Because I love my lanai.
What can I say I cannot lie.
It's a relaxing place to sit and read
Or just watch birds fly in and out of trees.
We added a bird cage and a spa
Should that be against the law?
It's a natural way to de-stress
To just relax and forget the mess.
Because of COVID I had to stay at home
So I spent a lot more time all alone
Sitting on my lanai.
And now I ask why
Didn't I appreciate it before?
Now I love it so much more.
Being happy and content is a choice
Get rid of the negative and rejoice
So you can just learn to let it go
And remember that God is in control.

Peace in Times of Trouble

We all want comfort in times of sorrow
Hoping for a return to peace by tomorrow.
Confronted with turmoil is difficult to face
Feeling helpless and in need of a warm embrace.
We desire rest when we are weary.
Someone to dry our eyes when they are teary.
Looking for healing in times of sickness and disease
Someone to turn to for relief and a quick reprieve.
When suffering strikes we have a decision to make.
We can turn to God knowing He will not forsake.
We will then find solace, solidity, tranquility and joy
Not anger, bitterness, rage and despair that will destroy.
We have been frightened and thrown off course this year.
It is no wonder that we are so filled with angst and fear.
Draw strength from God who provides peace in times of
    trouble.
Just ask and He will answer and be there for you on the
    double.

Chapter 13:

High on Dancing

High on Dancing

Dancing often is considered to be an antidote
Similar to a metaphor or an inspiring quote.
It acts as an exotic elixir,
Mood enhancer or problem fixer.
A concoction of patterns, movements, and steps
Is choreographed into a dance that may be simple or complex
Creating an effect like a drug or specialty medicine
Except with only positive side effects by comparison.
Dancing is a remedy for complacency and lethargy
Ironing out stress and tension to increase levels of energy.
Dancing as exercise bolsters physical and mental health
As it eases anxiety, sharpens the mind, and improves stealth.
A side benefit is how it builds friendships and social bonds
While it develops aerobic power like a magic wand.
If you get high on dancing losing yourself in the beat
And start expressing yourself with your arms and feet
Eventually your movements will transcend and be set apart
Especially when the dance emerges from within your heart.

The Language of Dance

Dance is the hidden language of body and soul.
The instrument is the body that has control
As it moves in time and space with a graceful force.
Later on a sense of muscle memory takes its course.
A dancer will ignite a light that begins to shine
Like chasing a dream that was left behind.
Dancers are like angels performing a twilight symphony
As if seeing a message in a bottle at the bottom of the sea.
Sometimes dancers express a mood of joy and happiness,
Or a more somber tone of sorrow and mournfulness.
A sequence of dance movements may be improvised
Or danced for a specific purpose as the story comes alive.
When the body moves and travels from one location to
    another
Dance becomes a language not written on a page like any
    other.
It can break linguistic barriers as the dancers take part
Opening up communication that comes from their hearts.

Barbara Welsh

Better When I'm Dancing

Dancing is a cure for the blues
It makes you feel like you're on a cruise
To a magical place where dreams come true
Where the sun shines all day and the sky is blue.

Dancing is the medicine that cures your soul
Your heart rejoices as your story unfolds
Using your hands and feet to make it complete
As you lose yourself in the music and the beat.

Fast and slow with a full turn left then right
Life is better when dancing every day and night.
Scissor and coaster steps done on all four walls
Helps to keep your mind sharp and on the ball.

Jazz boxes, twists and sailor steps all in a row
Just be sure you don't step on your own toe.
You are dancing with angels it may sometimes seem
When the patterns resemble a gentle flowing stream.

Maybe life is just a dance you learn and repeat
Helping your body to stay active and not retreat.
Life isn't perfect just like every dance you do
Some fit your style and are meant just for you.

You can add your own finesse and special flair
It is like a day you are at your best and love is in the air
Or when rain falls gently so flowers are refreshed
The way nature's wonder every day is expressed.

Dancing can take your mind away from problems
Lighten the mood as joy and hope now blossoms.
Dancing boosts self-esteem and sets you free
It provides many benefits you may never foresee.

Dancing with a Monster

If you dance with a ghost
You really can't boast.
No one will ever know
Because he really won't show.

If you moonwalk with a zombie
You might wind up in Miami
Falling into a very deep sleep
Waking up in a petrified heap.

Never dance with a ghoul
You'll soon look like a fool.
If you try doing the monkey
You will look way too funky.

If you dance with a goblin
You might start hobbling
While dancing the Flamenco in Spain
With a pain you won't want to explain.

Never dance with a beast
You could become his next feast.
If you dance the West Coast Swing
Your arm likely will end up in a sling.

If you dance with a vampire
You never know what he'll require
He might ask you to do the twist
Until you no longer exist.

Don't fall in love with a gorilla
Because you think he's Godzilla
When he asks you to tango
Do not call him Fernando.

So if you dance with a monster
To be safe, make sure it's an impostor
Dressed up in a scary Halloween costume
Like a black cat or a witch riding a broom.

Or try joining a flash mob of zombie-type killers
Performing a dance to Michael Jackson's "Thriller."
Could it be possible that monsters are often misunderstood?
They are fine dancers, rather friendly and intrinsically good.

Lola Baby

(This poem is dedicated to Lola Miller who is a fabulous dance teacher and friend.)

Her name is Lola
She was a drummer we are told.
Now a dance teacher who is supreme
Students feel they're appearing in a dream
Laughing and having fun while learning many dances
At the same time concentrating to make advances.
You are welcomed to class with the Good Morning Song
It makes you want to sing along
The first dance is the Happy Dance that starts the class
Ending with lots of giggles to make us laugh
To lighten your day and put you in a happy mood
We learn new dances while others are reviewed.
If it's your birthday be prepared to do the birthday dance
Learn the steps or fake it and do a little prance.
Lola will keep you on your toes
Never dull or boring as the music flows.
She gives us many clues to follow
So we never get lost or she may holler.
As an example, she might call "4 S's"
Meaning that 2 sailor steps and 2 shuffles is what comes next
Now no one will be perplexed.
If she says "sexy" we know what to do
If you come to class you'll learn it too.
"Put on the brakes" means time to stop
Don't keep going or try to hop.
If asked to remember a certain step like #6 or 7
It will be a clue that there's a hold or special step
As a reminder so you can prep.
When she raises her voice you know a restart is coming
Just in case your mind is slumming.
She calls the corners dings
It really is one of many things.

You need to be aware when she says "the singer leaves the
    stage"
It means a restart is coming or maybe a bonus so you can
    engage
She names the walls so you remember where you are
Like at Captiva, on your right is the fishy wall
Or the Roger wall you will recall.
Some walls are named after one of the students
Like the Bruce or Connie wall; don't dispute it.
Of course there is the back wall
Or the front wall is called Lola, that's her call.
Johnny is often asked to call it out
Like "sexy rocking chair" or "prissy walks 2," he tries to shout
She tells us not to look down at the floor
Smile and look up and it will show much more.
Don't just move your feet but use some pizazz
It will look better adding a little jazz.
Styling makes all the difference and endings are important
Dances look better with a finale of many assortments
Like saying done at the end of a dance called Done
Or pretending to take a sip of wine is another one
Or walking off the stage at the end of a dance
Making each dance look special to further enhance
Lola is happy when everyone dances in unison
Or when we loudly respond when she asks a question
If not, she might ask us to repeat the steps 13 times
We hope it doesn't happen or we will feel like mimes
Don't ever move when she is demonstrating, you soon will learn
It helps us to concentrate so we can repeat it when it is our turn
Pivot, pivot is different than walk, walk
We learn different dances doing our best not to talk.
She makes sure we know how to do a side rock, jazz box,
rocking chair, cross point, back rock, hinge turn, chasse left
or right, coaster step, scissor step, cross shuffle, back sweep,
behind side cross, kick ball, an oval vine or anchor step.
Before long you will know all these steps so you leave her
    class with lots of pep.

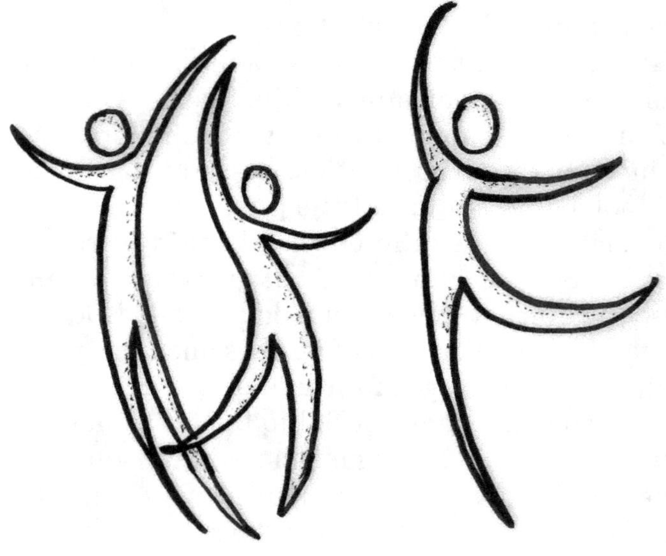

Dancing is Therapeutic

While dancing you often lose yourself and forget
Your problems, heartaches and any regrets.
The anxiousness that haunts you will disappear
As you learn a new dance and your mind starts to clear
Of all extraneous thoughts and worries that distract
Freeing you to focus on the steps and stay on track.
Dancing can be an energetic social expression
Making new friends and connections is an added dimension.
No matter the intensity, dancing helps to improve flexibility
Increase stamina, strengthen bones and improve mobility.
Dancing releases endorphins that may even boost your
    memory
Improving balance, coordination and augmenting energy.
There is an emotional element that is unique and a
    divergent part
Performing a dance not only with the body but with the heart.
So go ahead and dance like no one is watching; what harm
    can it do?
You will be uplifted and everyone around is enlightened too.

Chapter 14:

Drink Your Tea Slowly

Drink Your Tea Slowly

Don't criticize or find fault before knowing the facts
Say something negative you will have to retract.
You could have made the same mistake
And it wasn't your decision to make.

Some people tend to turn a trivial thing into something
    much bigger
Passing it all around until it becomes today's new thriller.
Through gossiping and exaggeration,
Embellishing and applying dramatization,
A snowball effect takes place.
It soon becomes a potentially dangerous race
Building upon itself as it becomes larger
Forming a vicious cycle or merciless supercharger.

Why not be the one who spreads goodness around?
Sending out positive vibes that are much more profound,
Initiating a beneficial or virtuous cycle
Leading to optimism available for recycle.
This pattern may become encouragement for the soul
By creating inner peace and allowing you to stay in control.

The more you give out positively, the more you get back.
Smiling or saying a kind word will keep you on track.
Your thoughts have a frequency and a corresponding vibration
That attract similar frequencies within each situation.
Negative thinking attracts negative energy;
Whereas positive action starts an undeniable synergy.
Hence, drink your tea slowly and live in the moment
Enjoy its soothing effect as a form of atonement.
Slow yourself down in order to move forward.
As you gaze on a single piece of fruit picture an orchard.
Soon you'll develop a greater appreciation for life
Plus increased happiness and the absence of strife.
Enjoy watching the last sun-rays as they settle into the sea
As you savor the mellow taste of a sweet cup of tea.

Shoulda, Coulda, Woulda and What-ifs

Saying I should've, could've and would've enhances regrets.
These negativity monsters make it hard for you to forget.
If you continually ruminate about past actions or what-ifs,
You'll have to find new emoticons or a creative gif.
Focusing on lost opportunities cannot be healthy.
If you don't move on you'll never be spiritually wealthy.
Don't allow past bad decisions to continually haunt you.
You can't change the past but you can face the future anew.
Exciting new opportunities present themselves every day.
Lamenting over what could have been is not the best way
To look forward to living, loving and making a difference.
Worries and what-ifs hide in the shadow of your magnificence.
Life is like a time machine that only goes one way—forward.
Time travel is mythical; you can't rewind or go backwards.
God promises us He has plans for a hopeful future.
Memories are like bits of data saved on a computer
To be used as a reference but not always for joy.
Your destiny is already programmed for you to employ.
Be encouraged as you live each day with a purpose,
Blocking the negativity monsters from trying to resurface.

A Thousand Roads

I could take a thousand roads but only one leads back to you.
I lift my head and my heart to see before me all that is true.
Some roads may be winding and lead into darkness
Try to avoid those paved with regrets and patches of
    loneliness.
It's possible to come to a road filled with temptations at
    every turn
Best not to take this road either or you will then be forced
    to learn
That you are accountable for your own behavior and actions.
Don't allow anger to take control or you'll lose a lot of traction.
These things I have learned as I travelled along many
    different paths.
I have tried to avoid the pitfalls that lend to sensations of
    wrath.
As I traversed these roads, I met many friends along the way
When God is walking beside me I know I will never get lost
    or go astray
I look for the road with bright rays of hope shining from
    high above
To lighten my journey and direct me home to my one true
    love.

Light, Laughter, and Love

Always move slowly toward the light
So when the sun disappears into the night
You are assured it will rise again tomorrow
With a renewed purpose in which to follow.
A sunrise can boost your emotional state
After a full moon lights up the sky when it is late.
Try to move away from the darkness
Although clouds will appear regardless.
Doubt is seen as darkness in your eyes
Whereas uncertainty can be easily disguised.
It is like fog or a heavy mist
Blocking the sun even though it still exists.
The mist is sometimes thick and heavy like a blanket
A weather pattern not suited for an outside banquet.
Thunder involves a dark sky that brings loud rumblings
As lightning streaks through cloud-like dumplings.

Barbara Welsh

Love grows in the light of the sun
It brings laughter and unexpected fun.
A spontaneous laugh is like soup boiling over
It spreads joy like a walk in a field of grass and clover.
Laughter is considered the music of the soul
It can make you lose control.
Laughter is a perfect mood enhancer
Similar to a whimsical song and rhythmic dancer.
Love and laughter will smooth off the edges
So you don't fear walking on narrow ledges.
Love gives you strength to try once more
Helping you to get your boat to shore.
Love grows when hatred stops spreading
Looking forward to the future instead of dreading.
Love shows the world that the best is yet to come
When you believe that God's work has just begun.
Light and laughter helps you to make it through
But nothing else compares to God's love for you.

True Inspiration

A sudden brilliant creative or timely idea
Inspired by a divine influence we cannot define.
True inspiration transcends ordinary experiences and
limitations.
It propels a person from apathy to probability and innovation.
Transforming the way we perceive our own capabilities.
Believing we have many and new-found possibilities.
Thomas Edison once said genius is one per cent inspiration
And ninety-nine percent perspiration.
Moments of inspiration do not apply to normal logic
The senses are amplified and become ideologic
Creating a thrilling feeling along with a burst of energy and
    awareness
When one is inspired time disappears and becomes fearless.
Willing to take a daring leap towards something truly great.
Inspiration provides the stimulus to rise above the norm in
    order to create
Awakening God-given talents in us then giving the glory up
    to Him.
Discovering new opportunities by allowing us to go out on
    a limb.
Creativity and motivation are tools of inspiration in which
    to strive.
Transcending ordinary experiences by becoming braver and
    more alive.

Happiness is Simple

Always put God first so all else falls in line
Then look out for others and try to be kind.
Goodness matters, tolerance is important
Stay positive, let negative thoughts lie dormant.
You will get back as much as what you give
Happiness is simple when you learn how to live.
Complaining is never helpful or very much fun
Not only for you but for everyone.
Every day have an uncontrollable gut-felt laugh
It initiates smiles all around on your behalf.
Keep it simple and you'll be happier,
More energetic and much snappier.

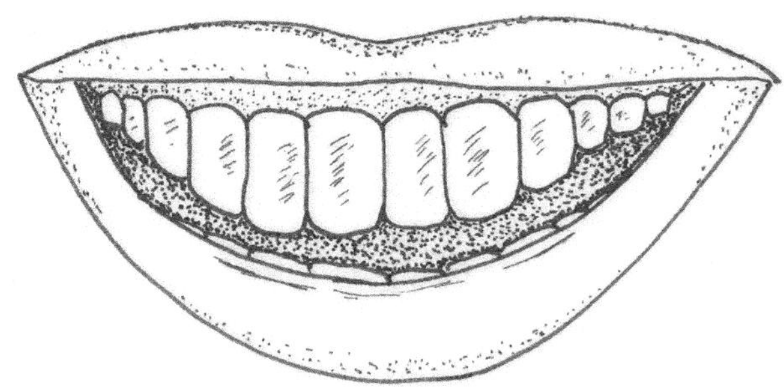

Chapter 15:

Raining Cats and Dogs

Barbara Welsh

Raining Cats and Dogs

Rain, rain go away
Come again some other day
Especially if today is your beach-side wedding
Or something needing an outdoor setting.
What if it really started raining cats and dogs?
Even worse if mixed with heavy smog and fog
But not as bad if it started raining toads and frogs.
Animals falling from the sky is an idiom century's old
Washed from roofs during stormy weather as is told.
If raindrops would keep falling on our heads
This idiom could take on a much different thread.
We've heard *when it rains it pours.*
Now will all these cats and dogs start causing a ruckus?
So we have to cover our heads with big brass buckets.
Will rainy-day friends come along and save the day?
Or fair-weather friends lead them all to go astray?
Problem solved; we realize *raining cats and dogs* is just an
    old-time saying
To rain unusually heavy is what they meant to be
    conveying.

Looking Through the Right Lens

Everyone is looking through a lens of some kind
That is how your vision and perception is designed.
You look through a lens of faith or one of fear
The one you wear is a result of what you see and hear.
Your choice decides how you perceive and live your life.
Seeing through a lens of fear causes unnecessary strife.
Whereas a lens of faith will guide you during a time of
    darkness
Helping you to thrive and survive in a world of harshness.
This lens serves as a corrective lens to see life more clearly
And to follow the right path and to love more dearly.
You also have access to the hand of God in times of crisis
Allowing you to focus on a purpose that is truly righteous.
Like a magnifying glass it enhances your spiritual vision
And facilitates clarity in making the right decisions.
You must narrow your vision to deepen your view
Filtering out the negative to see only what is true.
Looking through the lens of the world disguises your
    perception
Distorting your point of view triggering fraud and
    deception.
If you look at life through God's protective lens of love
You learn to listen to a voice resonating from up above
Correcting and filtering out any delusions and
misconceptions
As the world comes into focus without any earthly
    exceptions.

Barbara Welsh

Not a Fluke

Was it a stroke of good luck, a favorable break,
Just a fluke or simply a mistake?
When you almost have a fender bender
And you're sure the other guy was the offender.
Was it a fortunate chance occurrence,
Poetic justice or merely a coincidence?
Could it possibly be an answer to a prayer
That was said while you were unaware?
When things work out and you wonder why
Could it be due to a higher power you can't deny?
When God decides to bless you
And it all seems too good to be true
When situations come together in your favor
But you haven't demonstrated the best behavior.
When we or others decide to pray
God hears more than what we say.
He may answer more than we ask
Always there to complete the task
Giving more than what we can imagine
Causing miracles not random acts to happen.
In His own time and in His own way
It is never a fluke no matter what we say
Nor a silver lining or an aberration.
When we gather all the information
We find we haven't been duped
Because it really is **not a fluke!**

Extraordinary in the Ordinary

To take a breath each day is the ordinary
Sunrises and sunsets are more extraordinary.
Seasons change and time goes by just like playing a simple
    game.
Nothing in nature is stagnant; it's never mundane or stays
    the same.
Life is beautiful when you see the extraordinary in the
    ordinary
By searching, reaching out for glory and being exploratory.
God can make each day special and extraordinary
Marvelous and miraculous out of what's ordinary.
Trade in your pain and sorrow and replace it with joy.
If you think your life is falling apart it's hard to enjoy.
All that is happening around you and what lies ahead
Is God performing miracles so open your eyes instead.
Leave regrets and past mistakes behind.
God forgives and forgets, He is always kind.
Forgiveness is there for you.
There's nothing you have to do.
Just ask and your burdens will disappear
Never fear, He will not let them reappear.
God takes your ordinary life you're living now
And transforms it to extraordinary if you allow.
He becomes your ultimate and extraordinary friend
Like an anchor to hold you steady until the end.
When the ordinary will be forever released
Transformed into extraordinary harmony and peace.

Living on a Fault Line

Are you looking for a sense of stability in an unstable
    world
Where your emotions are being tossed, thrashed and
    swirled?
Do you wonder if you can handle another heartache
Or is this the gamble you have to make?
You may have been living on a fault line for too long
Crushing your dreams so you no longer feel strong.
When a fracture appears in the path you are taking
And there are unexpected changes causing you to feel
    forsaken
Try moving away from the fault line and its dangerous traps
To a place of safety where there is no impending collapse.
When the line between a smile and a frown is blurred
Blending into one until a tipping point has occurred
You might be fighting a villainous force
Making you believe that you have no other choice.
Look around for a bridge to take you to a place of hope
Away from the obstacles that lead to another slippery slope.
God will be there to lift you to secure and steady ground
Where a site of refuge exists and peace can be found.

Chapter 16:

Dream Catchers

A Web, Feathers, and Beads

A web, feathers and beads when connected together
Create a dream catcher or sacred loop
In the shape of a circle, it resembles a protective hoop.
According to legend, the air we breathe
Contains good and bad dreams
If you choose to believe
That when hung above the bed
The dream catcher attracts and catches
All your dreams and thoughts into the web
Good dreams pass through
Gently sliding down the feathers
To the sleeper below no matter the weather.
Bad dreams are caught in the web right away
Then disposed of in the light of day.
A bead may symbolize the spider...the web weaver itself
Weaving the web to trap dreams of good health.
Or the beads could simply represent
All the dreams that do not cause any harm
But couldn't pass through the web
Immortalized in the form of a sacred charm..
As a child, we said our prayers every night
Asking God to protect and hold us tight
As we grow, we become more aware
That God is our daily dream catcher
Not one that can be easily bought
But always there to counteract bad dreams and evil thoughts
The feathers are His hands that direct goodness and mercy
Toward us in order that we can fully comprehend and see
His offer for a personal relationship based on love
Smaller beads in the dream catcher represent blessings
Our perfect and predestined gifts
Sent to us with love from up above.

Trapped in a Gothic Horror Show

Am I trapped in a Gothic Horror Show?
Afraid to move, nowhere to go.
Am I a damsel in distress?
Should I be wearing a long black dress?
Am I lost in a gloomy horror episode
With intense emotions ready to implode?
Is Frankenstein lurking near
Or is it Dracula I should fear?
Witches, devils and mad scientists
Skeletons, scarecrows and a lioness
There are no heroes to be found.
It's too quiet, I can't hear a sound.
The atmosphere is shockingly cold.
Too scared, I'm not feeling very bold.
Will I see gruesome and scary misbehavior?
Should I call 911 to request a savior?
Monsters, ghosts and goblins are on display
Wake up, oh no, I forgot it's Halloween today.

Hopscotching

In just a few short months our country seems unrecognizable.
What happened to our one nation under God indivisible?
We're living in a country where we no longer feel safe.
The media is inciting fear in most every case.
Controlling our lives with false narratives
Asking us to agree with and believe their imperatives.
Are we hopscotching with the devil?
Is the scale tipped so it is no longer level?
If you disagree you're called a negative name
Seems like we're playing an unjust game.
Making a judgment before learning the facts
Feeling oppressed and not sure how to act.
Backbones are missing.
No one seems to be fighting back.
Moving erratically from place to place
Making it really hard to keep track
Like playing hopscotch on a crooked sidewalk
Skipping along quickly, trying to win, no time to talk.

Cheaters Never Win

Cheaters never really win
It becomes apparent in the end.
Winners never cheat even though they may lose.
Honesty and fairness is always what they choose.
Cheaters might feel good for a little while
But soon their conscience will be on trial.
Guilt sets in and gains made are soon erased.
Deceit eats at the soul and soon falls out of grace.
Many people try to correct mistakes in order to survive.
Sometimes lies carry on and fester when kept alive.
God forgives those who focus on personal repentance
Or the enemy takes control of the next questionable
   circumstance.
If God is not your ultimate guide
You will always live like you're trying to hide.
The end doesn't always justify the means
Evil lurks until you become no longer seen.
You decide between spending eternity in heaven or hell
Only time and your choices and decisions on earth will
   tell.

The Corridor

Take me down a corridor away from broken promises—
A narrow passageway independent and autonomous.
Staying on this path will lead to truth and honesty
To fend off hurtful words and harmful advice due to
    insecurity.
Make sure what you see, hear and read is good and true.
Avoid getting stuck in the fog clouding your point of view.
Pay careful attention to who and what you listen to
It will prevent inner turmoil from erupting and breaking
    through.
Pinpoint the source of discouragement you encounter.
Try to understand, don't judge, stay calm, don't flounder.
Process your emotions, use wisdom as a guide before you
    reply.
Social media can cause despair and reasons to question
    why.
Seek relief in forgiveness but be angered by injustice and
    malice.
Follow a course of righteousness that leads to your golden
    palace.
Stay faithful to your ideals and the purpose you have found
As the aesthetic aspects of true love will ultimately
    surround.

Cold Hearts and Sharks

Cold hearts and sharks are blindly insensitive
They usually are people who are overly argumentative.
You'll soon discover they are good at applying a double
   standard
But can't handle it when they are the ones being slandered.
When the shoe is on the other foot, they cower
Never caring about anyone but themselves and their power
Not afraid to destroy another life as they bask in the sunshine
Until someone takes a stand and finally draws a line.
You will be able to characterize them by their actions
So never be fooled by their words or other distractions.
Often, they live in a world of their own and what they require
Completely absorbed by their own thoughts, needs and desires
Showing little concern for the effects of their twisted morality
Uncaring until they bump up against reality.
Don't stoop to their level
Try to be kind and somewhat gentle
They may take note of the positive way you live and act
Noticing a purity and goodness they themselves lack.
Change can only take place one step at a time
With strength emanating from a force that is divine.

Chapter 17:

Two Sides to Every Coin

Two Sides to Every Coin

There are frequently two different viewpoints on every subject
Like two sides of a coin, why gamble on what viewpoint
    you select.
You can toss a coin and take a chance to which side it will
    land
Or try to figure out by learning the truth on which it does
    stand.

I have an example based on scientific fact
    An explanation researched to help keep you on track.
To scientifically explain how two natural phenomenons
    will act
Let's compare the differences between a tsunami and a
    tidal wave.
In nature it is difficult to understand and distinguish how
    each one behaves.
A tidal wave is a shallow water wave caused by
    gravitational interactions between sun, moon, and earth
A tsunami is an ocean wave triggered by earthquakes of
    great force
Occurring under the ocean according to the research.

Often confused and thought to be exactly the same
Both are waves but have different causes not always clearly
    relayed.
Weather patterns, like the news, may change and be
    different on any given day.
It is hard to interpret what they are saying so not to be led
    astray.

Intolerance of differing opinions or beliefs is a downfall we
  face.
Should schools remain closed or allowed to open at a slow
  pace.
Decisions should be made based on scientific and medical
  facts
So the wise conclusion sends young students back on the
  right track.

Too many people think their side is ultimate and their
  mind becomes closed.
They don't analyze using logic before making the
  conclusion they chose.
Like two sides of a coin you should not have to flip to win
  or lose.
A fact is a fact and shouldn't be misconstrued.
Truth is truth we have to conclude.

Prayer shapes your thinking and changes your perspective.
It helps to remain focused, stay on track and be more
  selective.
There is only one God, one side, and one basic truth
That is based on the Bible and only requires trusting in
  faith.

Barbara Welsh

Confetti or Spaghetti?

Confetti is composed of small pieces of paper or other material
Various colors rain down creating a little bit of delirium
Usually thrown at celebrations especially parades and
    weddings
If you like confetti, you are frivolous and enjoy party settings
You also like frills and adornments
You're lighthearted and make every day a performance.

Spaghetti is a long, thin, solid cylindrical noodle pasta
Similar to macaroni, ravioli, penne, and lasagna
A staple of traditional Italian cuisine
Delicious, nutritious and better than beans
If you like spaghetti, you prefer comfort
You're a really good sport
Enjoy breaking bread with a friend
You're sympathetic, being kind is your trend.

Confetti or spaghetti?
Would you rather throw some confetti
Or eat a big bowl of spaghetti?
Do neither or both
Say adios...
And head for the Serengeti!

We Don't Talk Anymore

Are we taking part in a texting frenzy?
Is it becoming the only way to be friendly?
Has sending a text now replaced
Talking to someone face to face?
A few quick words gets right to the point
Make it good so you won't disappoint.
Acronyms are used to save time
No personal touch, seems like a crime.
Has emailing lost its luster?
Is it due to being in a constant fluster?
Too much spam and junk mail to go through
You're now up to one thousand and two.
Phone calls are definitely used as a last resort
If you need to talk to someone make it short.
Your kids don't believe in voice mail
For them, leaving a message is beyond the pale.
When using the microphone it comes out all wrong
Spell check makes corrections that don't belong.
You just called your best friend a whaaat
Too late now you sound like a nut.
When texting, mistakes are easily made.
Sending before proofing gets you dismayed.
Uh oh, you sent a text to the wrong person
Or worse to an 8-person thread for dispersion.
You accidentally hit send a little too soon
It doesn't make sense, you feel like a goon.
Then you hit delete instead of send
Or send when you should delete; when will it end?
Writing a letter is really a thing of the past
That ship has sailed and the die has been cast.

Your Pep 'R Upper

If you feel lonely and sad
Call your pep 'r upper
You will surely be glad.
Down in the dumps
Call your pep 'r upper
Soon you'll feel like jiving and jumping.
We all need to laugh and smile
Uplifted at least for a little while.
Is there someone in your life that brings you cheer?
Your day is made brighter whenever they are near.
It may be a friend, a spouse or even a pet.
Call your pep 'r upper and you'll be all set
Then you can do the same for someone else
No longer will you feel like an elf-on-the-shelf.
By uplifting one another, the happier we all will be
Just be someone else's pep 'r upper and you'll see
What goes around comes around...
The unity we are seeking can surely be found.

Toppers

Almost everyone knows or has met a topper.
Known for telling tales that turn into whoppers.
A topper is a person who responds to hearing someone
　　else's story
Then tells a similar story but more fantastic, filled with
　　personal glory.
They've done everything you have but more often and
　　much better
Filled with exaggerated and overstated details right down
　　to the letter.
You might say,"I dislocated my knee when dancing at the
　　square."
The topper says,"Yeah, well I broke my leg in four places
　　dancing there."
You might say,"I met Taylor Swift before the concert and
　　got her autograph."
The topper says, "So, I went backstage, we talked, then
　　snapped her photograph."
Extreme toppers can drive you crazy.
You try to avoid them by acting dazy.
Maybe toppers just need attention and are insecure.
Wish I knew what to do then I'd be first to find a cure.

Chapter 18:

Finger-Pointing & Stone-Throwing

Finger-pointing and Stone-throwing

Casting or assigning blame for something on or to someone
 else
Like saying "my sister broke the vase" when it really was
 yourself.
Finger-pointing is often an effort to deflect blame.
Harmful and inconsiderate it's not a nice game.
Making false accusations when you are to blame.
A cowardly act that should create a feeling of shame.
Unfortunately it happens all the time by people in power.
Unprofessional scrutiny of others as an attempt to overpower.
An unwise decision because when you point one finger at
 another
There are 3 fingers pointing back at you showing your own
 true color.
Stone-throwing or judging is another way of showing lack
 of respect.
A selfish and thoughtless reaction that produces a negative
 effect.
The Bible says "who is without sin shall cast the first stone."
Only those who are blameless have a right to judge on their
 own.
When you judge others you dim your own light.
A finger-pointer or stone-thrower is a disgraceful sight.
Perhaps they're scared of somebody else achieving something
That they can only dream of being able to achieve or to swing.
Feeling like a failure they react by pointing their finger
Or throwing a stone and thinking that they are the winner.

FOMO Promos

FOMO is rampant today.
If you have it, don't run away.
It's an early 21st-century abbreviation for fear of missing out.
What is causing this phenomenon; if you know please
    shout it out.
So what is FOMO?
And what are its causes or promos?

Promo 1—Social media websites
Can cause anxiety or the syndrome "fight or flight."
Fifty-six percent of social media users are victims
Creating envy and frustration, it's an effective system.
It's a social media-manufactured emotion
As a new word in the dictionary it's causing quite a
    commotion.

Promo 2—Facebook
Is guilty because when you take a look
You constantly want to check so you're caught by its hook.
Because it looks like everyone else's life is so perfect
If yours doesn't measure up, it can have a negative effect
That can cause you to feel depressed
Often overwhelmed and very stressed.
Thinking you might miss an opportunity for some social
    interaction
Friends having a good time without you could be your
    reaction.

Promo 3—Smart phones
Enable you to remain in close contact so you never feel alone
Texting and compulsive checking for status updates on
    your phone
Creating a good or bad reaction to set the daily tone.

Promo 4—Written material
Such as newspapers, newsletters and catalogs with lists of
    things to do
Offering an endless stream of information and ways to
    change your view.

Promo 5—The mainstream media
Including TV, news broadcasts, radio talk shows, and
    podcasts
It is all coming at you way too fast
So you ask, how long will this fear continue to last?

Promo 6—Friends and Peer Pressure
Create apprehension that you are not in the know
You're out of touch socially and have nothing to show.
A fear that others are having a much better time without you
Festers until you think something is wrong so what do you do?

Promo 7—Shoulditis
Means trying to please others and not thinking about
    yourself
Hiding your true feelings by putting them away on a shelf
Always saying yes, not knowing how to say no to a request
Getting mad at yourself because you really wanted to rest.

So now you may be saying Oh no!
Do I have FOMO?
Settle down it isn't fatal, you have the control
Analyze your daily actions and see how it goes
Consider if any of these FOMO promos
Need to be put into slow-mo
Be honest with yourself to see if you are afraid of missing out
Then decide which ones you can limit or just strike them out.

One-way Ticket

Did you make an unfortunate mistake?
Buy a ticket that went only one way
Now you feel cheated and have nothing to say
You didn't know you were headed to station #1984.
It must be a bad dream; you're not really sure.
Can't get a refund or even say what's on your mind
If you disagree, the regular passengers are not very kind.
Before you arrive you're forced to keep repeating a lie
Pretend you believe it; try not to look them in the eye.
Why did this happen you ask every day.
It's like a horror show in most every way.
Things are changing so fast nothing seems right
You have to find a way to fight back
When there are no return tickets in sight.
The only way out is with some help from above
Replace all this hate with truth and a whole lot of love
You pray God will intervene and step in at last
Come to your rescue so you can go back to the past
Try not to look at the troubles that are arising
They're beyond your control it's not so surprising
Fix your eyes on what you cannot see
Don't wonder how this can really be
Stop focusing on the things you cannot change
Although you wish you could at least rearrange
They will soon all be gone
And what you do not see now
Will last forever like a prophetic song.

Pass-it-on Hysteria

Did you ever play the game called pass it on?
Similar to when you pass a baton
This game starts when one person whispers a phrase
Passing it from one person to the next without delay
Until it has passed around a circle several times
The phrase should be at least two or more lines
The last person tells what he or she just heard
Then the first person repeats their original words.
The result is usually two very different versions
Like the media's attempt to create diversions
Fear and hysteria is created and spread all around
Exaggerations and untruths can now be found
Feeding on itself until it is becomes out of control
Pass-it-on hysteria is now on a roll
Creating psychological disorders and stress
Leading to anxiety, irritability and nervousness
Triggering uncontrollable worry, agitation and feelings of
    desperation
Today's media likes to excite without a plausible explanation
They must be self-centered, vain, and craving of attention
Markedly manipulative hoping for a hysterical sensation.
Self-righteousness and hypocrisy are twins that go together.
Each feeds the other so judging is the poison that pits one
    against another.
How about playing pass-it-on confidence and calmness?
And pass-it on forgiveness, togetherness and a feeling of
    oneness.

Chapter 19:

Forgiveness

Forgiveness

Forgiveness is the sweet words of goodness coming from
    our lips
Extending mercy to those who offend us if they slip.
The mind may not forget but the heart has the power to
    forgive.
It is the only way to exist in harmony and to live.
If you hold anything against anyone you should forgive them.
Best to forgive their transgressions and not condemn.
Look deeply into yourself to offer it, no strings attached.
A voluntary action with gradual healing will be dispatched.
It's difficult whether you are giving or receiving forgiveness.
A two-way street that softens hearts enhancing spiritual
    fitness.
To forgive is powerful; showing love as a gift given to a friend.
The Bible offers guidance to promote healing so lives can
    mend.
Forgiveness establishes remission, harmony and restoration
No longer bound and lost in a state of isolation.
Love speaks louder than hurt feelings in today's world
Where wanting revenge seems to be what is preferred.
The need for retaliation can poison your mind.
It takes courage just to let go and be kind.
Forgiveness is an attribute of those who are strong
Providing emotional relief so how can it be wrong.
When you forgive it will set the prisoner free
Only to discover that you are that prisoner; you'll soon see.
Forgiveness liberates the victim; it's a funny thing
It warms the heart and calms the sting.
There is no love without forgiveness
And no forgiveness without love
Available as a gift offered to each and everyone
Who believes in God's redeeming love from high above.

Age is Only a Number

You've heard the saying, *you're only young once.*
*Dr. Seuss also has said: you're only **old** once!*
Some might say to themselves, *I'm too young to be this old.*
Or say to you, "you look so good for your age."
Do they mean you'd look better if you stood in a cage?
At this time in your life you will make many new friends.
Each one has a name that ends in *ist; seems like a trend.*
They could include an orthopedist, urologist, rheumatologist,
Pulmonologist, dermatologist, and allergist to name a few.
Needing glasses to read and see at a distance is now
   something new.
Is your hearing getting murkier; you're becoming deafer
   than a door nail?
You go in a room and forget what you came in for, to no avail.
You try intermittent fasting and cutting out carbs to lose a
   few pounds
Start counting calories and points or a new fad that's going
   around.
White pill in the morning, blue at night; will the next be a
   cute zebra stripe?
New treatments, liniments and CBD products are getting so
   much hype.
Oh my, let's change this to a positive and flip it around.
Age is just a number, a new way to look at it can be found.
How about the 60 minutes of aerobics you do every day
Like Zumba, line dance, and spinning classes or trying
   something new?
Seniors and baby boomers swim, bike, jog, walk, hike and
   play billiards too.
Golf, tennis, pickleball, volleyball, and softball games are
   on the list.
Pilates, ballet, yoga, bocce, beach tennis, horseshoes you
   get the gist.
A goal of 10,000 steps; as our trackers and Fitbits confirm
   and support.
To verify that age really is only a number and still remain a
   good sport
Try saying this rallying cheer each day if you so dare
Raise your arm, shake your fist and say *no one knows and I
   don't care!*
Then be thankful for what you can do and add a heartfelt prayer.

The Lightning Round

If this is the lightning round of your life
Then take action now with a goal in sight.
Your bucket list still has many items to go.
Believe in yourself, you're more competent than you know.
Focus on the outcome not the obstacles you face.
The odds you give yourself are what matters to finish the race.
You can accomplish whatever your mind chooses to believe.
Stop putting things off, there is plenty yet to achieve.
You are the best that you will ever be
Fearless and unstoppable; it is easy to see.
The world will adjust, you have nothing to hide.
All things are possible when God is your guide.
Ready, set, go…
Win, place or show
This is your lightening round
Where God's love will astound.

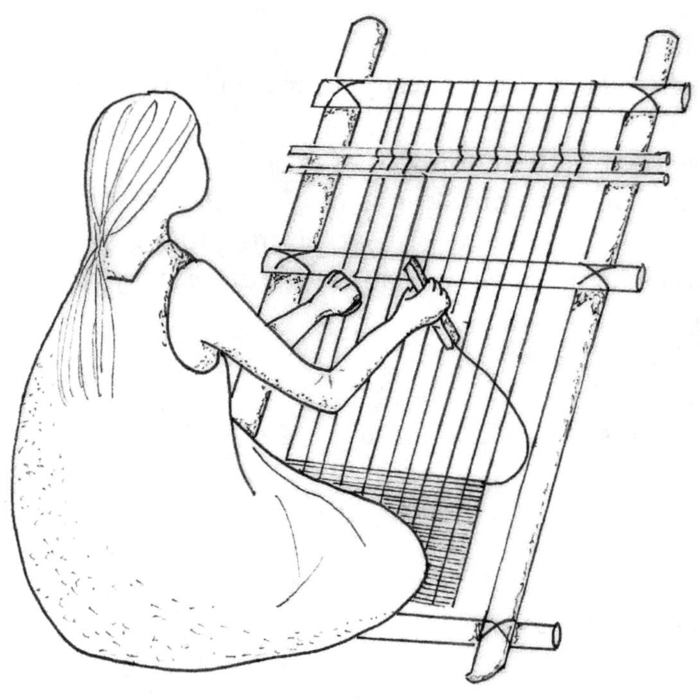

Our Life's Tapestry

A tapestry can be an intricate combination of things
Or sequence of events that the future brings.
When a picture of us is projected for others to see
It consists of all the threads that make up our life's tapestry
Weaving together past events, relationships and encounters
Displaying it to people in our lives so that it may empower.
God creates each person with a spiritual tapestry that is blank
An individual life starts when God chooses a single thread
    from His bank
Then weaves it together into a unique blueprint that forms
    in the womb
To be manifested when it is the right time for the blossom
    to bloom.
A tapestry metaphor creates a beautiful imagery
That conveys how the individuality of every person's
    symmetry
Comes together with culture in a harmonious and
    unexpected way
Experiences weave together as personality and character
    come into play.
The variety of threads creates a beautiful one-of-a-kind pattern
Showcased to the world like the glow of a multicolored
    lantern.
It moves forward on a long journey to fulfill life's purpose
As the intricacies of our tapestry come into view and
    slowly surface.

Chapter 20:

Rough Seas Ahead

A Stormy Sea

When waves come crashing down upon you
Tossing you all around; up, down to-and-fro
Caught in the undertow of a stormy sea
And lost in the darkness as you try to break free
You must swim with all your might towards the light
No matter how rough the sea you can fight to make it right.
Life's toughest storms prove the strength of your anchor
That keeps you focused and away from all the daily rancor.
Every ocean has a shore, every challenge has an end
During the most difficult times, stay strong, do not bend.
The human heart is like a ship on a stormy sea
Rough seas make stronger sailors you will agree.
Plans and desires can swiftly change direction
But God offers you a lifeboat as a shield of protection.
If you have faith and persevere through difficult times
Life becomes more cherished in the heart that it enshrines.

A Rough and Rocky Road

Sometimes a rough and rocky road
Can take you to a beautiful place
No pain, no gain and step by step
Will take you there not demanding an arduous pace.
A day can seem so hard if you focus on what can go wrong.
Don't let negative thoughts dominate your mind for long.
Before you know it you're standing on shaky ground
So you think there's no hope or an easy way to be found.
A few rocks and pebbles along with a little rubble
Keeps you on guard and away from a lot of trouble.
Your journey may take you on a bumpy ride
Focus on a destination that will provide you with pride
Take advantage of a divinely inspired GPS
Then there will be no need to have to guess
Live your life with **Grace**
Pray often
Follow a loving **Savior**
So that rough and rocky road you travel
Will not cause you to unravel
It will take you where you long to be
Where blessings are obvious for you to see.

Harmony or Heartbreak

Don't be conflicted by your own bitterness
Get acquainted with the secret of forgiveness
Carrying around hurts and resentment from the past
Destroys harmony and healthy relationships that will last.
Harmony in music is the combination of simultaneous
    musical notes
Like comforting Biblical or philosophical quotes.
Harmony in dance occurs when the beat coincides
With each step that a dancer takes
Coordination of each movement that he or she makes.
Harmony in relationships is when people live together
    peacefully
Rather than fighting, arguing or acting selfishly.
The opposite of harmony
Is dissonance or disharmony
Leading to headache and overwhelming distress
Possibly even heartbreak and unavoidable stress.
It takes a strong heart to unconditionally love someone
Especially if you are afraid it will eventually come undone
It takes a stronger heart to continue to love after being hurt
The trust you once had is gone and emotions go on alert.
In music, disharmony is unpleasant to the ear.
In dance, getting out of step with the beat is a dancer's
    greatest fear.
The secret is to try to maintain harmony
To avoid heartache and circumvent strife
Like in melodious music, elegant dances and all other
    aspects of life.

Faith to Move a Mountain

I hold my cross of gold in my hand
To ask for help and improve my stand
Praying for hope for tomorrow
And compassion to ease the sorrow.
Help me to rise above the norm
To find shelter from this raging storm
Looking for a sky that is clear and blue
Keeping my focus on only what is true.
With my eyes always on the ball
To avoid losing and causing a fall
I believe that I will never be alone
Although there is still so much unknown.
Worry only weighs a person down
So I ask that faith remains and stays around
To erase the doubts that cross my mind
So they will dissolve and be left behind.
As these mountains move slowly into the sea
I know that God is in control of what lies ahead for me.

The Wounded Heart

When your wounded heart is in need of healing
It never will when there is something you are concealing.
If you have been offended don't allow it to take root
Only to become a prisoner within the walls you have built.
You may emerge as someone who is judgmental and proud
Not willing to admit you're walking under a dark cloud
Wounded and in need of restoration—
A perfect recipe for hatred and disassociation.
Take your pain out of the shadows and into the light
With some soul searching it will come into sight
Propelling you to relinquish what you are withholding
As you release the shame you will feel emboldened
Lifting the burden of guilt that you have shouldered.
A heart can mend completely according to your faith
Trusting and believing will create your own sincerity domain.
As sadness wanes, love is restored and anger no longer is
   pending
The anguish will slowly fade away resulting in a happier
   ending.
Rainbows always appear after a bad storm according to
   God's design
Reminding us that there is always hope and light after a
   difficult time.

Chapter 21:

The Potter's Wheel

The Potter's Wheel

We are the clay
You are the potter
Mold me after you
Trusting in your craft
Waiting for your final draft
Spin me into what you want me to be
Your handiwork for all to see.

A potter's wheel is a machine that makes clay take shape
Trimming the excess to create a form not easy to escape.
Rings of color are added to beautify the finished form
From clay to object sturdily made to weather any storm.
Jeremiah is instructed to go to the potter's house to learn a
    lesson.
The potter turns the wheel with his foot to mold and make
    the vessel.
The piece was flawed while still in his hands so he decides
    to make another.
If we as a nation turn to evil, the potter's choice will be
    easy to uncover
To choose between allowing redemption, reconstruction or
    destruction
Mercy will prevail if we reform our evil ways and listen to
    instruction
Two factors determine the outcome imposed on us today
The skill of the potter and the condition of the clay.
Sooner or later we're going to find ourselves in the potter's
    hands.
Discipline is another word for refinement as the new
    product stands.
Remove impurities from our lives now and change our ways
Or face destruction and perhaps the end of all our days.

In Today's World

Today's world seems upside down
Because truth is nowhere to be found.
In today's world, we are moving backwards
As we face a society with so many distractions.
Every day we experience the bitter taste of doubt
Influenced by social media spread throughout.
We are easily distracted by our material possessions
That impact our lives by turning into daily obsessions.
Everywhere we turn we're bombarded by various ads
Promising a better life if we fall for the latest new fad.
Hearing these messages over and over makes it hard to resist
The temptation to pursue so the opportunity won't be missed.
If our possessions lead us to always wanting more
A point will be reached when there is nothing left to score.
We tend to lose focus on what is really important
So what should matter most in our lives lies dormant.
Sound decisions, trust and belief in God take second fiddle
Problems arise as we begin to feel empty and bitter.
Remove yourself from this daily ritual of self-focus
And bask in the serenity of a new life void of neurosis.
Be comforted by a fresh bubbling spring that soothes from
    within
Leading to a glorious new world where forgiveness begins.

Brave and Courageous

To stay brave and courageous is not easy
Especially when life is not so happy and breezy.
You start feeling sorry for yourself like you're all alone
As each new day becomes filled with more of the unknown.
When someone you love can't seem to catch a break
And your heart gets hit by a rock increasing the ache.
This should be the time to be strong and stand tall
Face what is insurmountable head on and not fall.
As a new dimension of pain is piercing your heart
You want to yell and scream without falling apart.
Allowing the anger inside to bubble up and seep out
Will only increase frustration spreading more doubt.
Despondency will increase if you don't snap out of it
Try not to be afraid, have courage and don't submit
To the forces of evil that lead to hopelessness and despair
It may seem unfair if you look around and start to compare.
Many highs and lows are a part of life's pattern and design
Always be excited for others when it's their time to shine.
Psalm 27 encourages us to wait patiently on the Lord
To be brave and courageous and live within His accord.
Your heart will not be afraid while maintaining confidence
In the power and protection of His divine providence.

It's Good to Know

There is a bright light that glows
Whenever hope breaks through
Because of a friend like you.
Someone who lifts you up when you fall
Always answers when you call.

It's good to know...
You have a friend to hold your hand.
Is there to catch you when you land
Willfully sacrificing precious time
Never selfish nor unkind.

It's good to know...
The feeling of sunshine on your face
With a love that time can't erase
Acting as a soft wind beneath your wings
That is what true friendship brings.

It's good to know…
That your faithfulness stretches to the sky
You are blessed and don't know why
Easing fears by showing you a little kindness
A light that shines brightly through the darkness.

It's good to know…
You have someone who fills your cup to the top
Encourages you not to stop
Acts as a bridge between the gaps
To help avoid life's harmful traps.

It's good to know…
You have a friend who halts your defenses
Brings you back to your senses
Gives you strength to carry on once more
Isn't that what love is for?

Barbara Welsh

Another Heart

Sometimes I wish I had a heart that doesn't break
Along with another one to absorb all the heartache.
One heart feels only tenderness and love
Because it is managed and controlled from up above.
When facing a situation in which I have no control
I take a deep breath and drift along with the flow.
When it's out of my hands and I'm just treading water
I think what if this heart is made of brick and mortar
It will surely sink to the bottom without a trace
Then my other heart is available to take its place
Restored, mended and no longer broken into pieces
Where God's love envelopes and protection increases.
A heart may cry on the inside but if equipped with a
    protective shield
It will not break apart, surrender or ever yield
To whatever life throws because ahead are brighter days
Where the sun is shining through the fading haze.

Chapter 22:

Hold It up to The Light

Hold It Up to the Light

A branch cannot produce fruit by design
Especially if it is severed from the vine.
From the beginning every beating heart
Connects to a lifeline from which it cannot part.
The purpose of life is not just to live and die
But to stay anchored and not to question why.
Always look for and be inspired by the truth
Forced to trust without seeing any proof.
The wind blows but you can only feel its effect
It can't be ignored but is worthy of respect.
God's magnificence may be beyond your comprehension
But when held up to the light It is worthy of your attention.
While here on earth there is a purpose to your existence
So forgive and love unconditionally without resistance.
Moments in each season when held up to the light
Will show you when the time is right
To let go and move on with eyes wide open
As you leave hope for tomorrow with words unspoken.

Entertaining Angels

You can walk right past an angel and not be aware
They don't look any different and won't give you a scare.
So be kind and hospitable to everyone including a stranger
It's possible you have made contact with a real-life angel.
Be careful how you treat people you don't really know
They may be part of God's plan that you choose to forgo
Helping you in ways that are hard to anticipate.
Stay aware, be willing and ready to participate
By offering help to those who have been mistreated
So you continue to make a difference that is easily
repeated.
Open your heart to those who are vulnerable
As you selflessly give, it no longer feels uncomfortable.
God instructs us to listen and love one another
Showing compassion as you would to a sister or brother.
Don't judge others, that is God's job to do
God will never fail or abandon you.
Fight the evil forces that exist in this world
In order for goodness and mercy to be unfurled.
You never know when an angel is near
Soon their presence will become very clear.

Your Finest Hour

This could be your finest hour, your greatest day
Your place in time so don't throw it away
A defining moment so be ready to shine
Focusing on your strengths that will define
An event that surpasses all expectations
Leading to many extraordinary revelations
Such as something life changing that brings joy
When you meet your newborn grand-baby girl or boy
Or it could be something less profound but significant—
The night you danced like a star and were magnificent
The day you got to be a part of your son's TV show
Or when you became "engaged" and are now all aglow
The time you ran your best time in a marathon or 10K race
Published a book and signed them at a special place
Mastered a piece of music until it was the perfect blend
Celebrated your birthday with very special diva friends
Spent quality time this summer with grandkids and family
These are the best times so live each day harmoniously
This could be your finest hour, your greatest day, your
   place in time
And with God by your side there's no mountain you cannot
   climb.

Insights of the Wise

Learning to do what is right, just and fair
From the knowledge and wisdom of teachers who care.
Written a long time ago, Proverbs provide a gateway to truth
A book of instruction and inspiration for your own
    personal use.
No need to buy self-help books and instructional DVDs
When there is all that you need in each chapter and verse.

The theme of Proverbs is stated in chapter 1, verse 7, it is
    not in disguise
Only when a person trusts in God will they be truly wise.

Wise choices will watch over you, understanding keeps you
    safe.
As stated in Proverbs Chapter 2, verse 11, solid advice
    given in every case.

You'll find 31 chapters full of good examples and
    instructions all in one place
Study, reflect, take your time as you read at your own
    comfortable pace.

In chapter 18, verse 19 we are warned what should not ensue:
Spouting off before listening to the facts is both shameful
	and foolish to do.

In chapter 20, verse 29 we are told:
The glory of the young is their strength;
The gray hair of experience is the splendor of the old.

This is just the tip of the iceberg when it comes to what's
	in store.
The book of Proverbs is an instruction manual for life plus
	so much more.
Open a Bible, you'll be surprised and enlightened if you
	read a little each day.
It will alter the way you look at your life in most every way.
It's a Bible revival I heard Pastor Norman say
He calls it the happy book when you can look at it that
	way.

Internet Addicts

At what point does daily screen time become really too
  much?
Is it when it takes control of your time and becomes too
  much of a crutch?
It's been proven that it can become a serious social
  addiction
Resulting in stress and anxiety; a recent psychological
  prediction.
Research has shown that overuse of social media can affect
  the brain
Leading to a compulsive pattern of use that becomes a real
  drain.
Constantly checking on social media sites can get out of
  control.
Reading texts and sending replies, oh no now you're really
  on a roll.
Maybe it's time to set some boundaries before it starts
  taking its toll.

Try visiting only social media sites that will add value to
  your life.
Otherwise you feel agitated and angry giving you additional
  strife.
Like food, make healthy choices, use social media less
  often especially before bed.
Disconnect for an hour or more, read a book, have a
  discussion instead.
Starting a digital diet or detox can prove beneficial for
  energy renewal
Turn off notifications, take a walk, have a real conversation
  to refuel.
What did we do before smart phones and tablets consumed
  so much of our time?
Less stress, headaches, worries, hurt feelings, loneliness;
  weren't we just fine?
Disconnect to reconnect should be a new motto and pattern
  to follow.
Be bold, less controlled, and use restraint before becoming
  a desperado.

Chapter 23:

Can You Teach a Pig to Sing?

Can You Teach a Pig to Sing?

Can you teach a pig to sing?
Only with an oink that has a special ring.
Pigs squeal but can they carry a tune?
No, but don't make them mad or they'll start to swoon.
Can you teach a pig to dance?
Maybe if you start with a simple prance.
This exercise may frustrate both you and the pig
Unless you decide to do just a little jig.
Can you teach a zebra how to paint
With subtle colors so he won't faint?
If the zebra can paint between the lines
It will give him a brand new way to shine.
Can you teach a platypus to whistle
Without leading to a sudden class dismissal?
A platypus has a mouth with an unusual shape
That won't allow musical notes to escape.
So this endeavor will not work
Don't try it unless you want to be a jerk.
So what if the shoe is on the other foot—
You meet a chicken who wants to use his how-to book
To try to teach you the chicken dance
If you're brave enough to take the chance.
Then a rabbit appears ready to teach the bunny hop
Which turns into so much fun you don't want to stop.
Who says you can't teach an old dog new tricks?
I just learned how to play Pick-Up Sticks.

Animal Wishes

I wish I could be a lovely mermaid today
So I could swim, flip my tail and make a big spray.

No I'd rather be a butterfly so I can fly
Up in the air and feel a natural high.

Or how about a friendly monkey
And jump around and swing free in a tree.

A cute little turtle
Never has to wear a girdle.

I think I'd like to be a hippopotamus
Then I'd never have to sweep or dust.

How about I turn into a bright pink flamingo
Dance on one leg and do an eye-candy type tango.

If I could be a kitty cat
I wouldn't have to worry if I got fat.

A little pig could be quite a gig
I could hop around and do the jig.

Being an antelope
Could give me some hope
And I wouldn't feel like such a dope.

If I were a camel with a very tall neck
I'd be allowed to say oh what the heck.

A platypus would be something very unique
With my duck bill I would look very sweet.

If I could be a fluffy cute little rabbit
I would be able to keep all my bad habits.

A lime green frog can jump around and leap
But somewhere I heard they have smelly feet.

Being a peacock would surely steal the show
My beautiful feathers would make me all aglow.

Wish I could be a big fuzzy bear
Then surely I would not have a care.

Or if I became a fly on the wall
I would be able to tell it all.

I wish I could fly up in the sky so blue
Just like a lovely bird can do.

So what animal would you like to be
Add on a few lines so we all can see.

Acknowledgments

Debbie Campana

My awesome, dedicated editor and friend who has read, critiqued and edited every poem in this book. Without her none of these poems wold have come to fruition.

Phyllis Schechtman

My proof reader and friend who reads and approves all of my poems. She is my cheerleader and lends a hand whenever needed.

My Family

My husband, Michael, who supports me every step of the way and also my children and grandchildren, which includes Jennifer Caldwell, Stephen Caldwell, Andrew Caldwell and their spouses, Peter Farah, Liberty Caldwell and Stephanie Caldwell, and eight grandchildren: Nyah, Layla, Kira, John, Finely, Evelyn, Hudson, and Quinn.

My Forever Friends and Pep 'R Uppers

Debbie, Phyllis, Bonnie, Pat, Valerie, Carol, Jean and Judy also known as the Dancing Divas who inspire me to keep writing.

All My Dancing Friends and Teachers

Wanda, Rachel, and Kelly from the Pregnancy and Family Care Center

College Friends:

Barbara Romine — Foreword
Sheila Rossi—"The Fragility of Life"
Joanne Fischer—"A Clock Named Joanne"

Maryjean (Jeanie Nagel)—in loving memory of a friend and co-counselor at the Pregnancy and Family Care Center, October 25, 1939 - April 3, 2023. "The Forever Friend"

About the Author

Barbara C. Welsh is a poet, editor, and retired teacher among many other accomplishments.

She started writing poetry during the COVID-19 pandemic. She was learning a new dance on line when she wrote her first poem called "Hoping, Praying, and Dancing." Since then she has written over 360 poems, many of which have been published in *The Villages Daily Sun*, *Poet's Corner* and *The Village Neighbors Magazine*. Her first book, "One Bright Day" was published in 2022 and is sold on Amazon.com, Barnes & Noble.com, and Walmart.com.

Barbara loves to dance, especially line dancing, Zumba, and more recently, cardio drumming. She was in the Gemstone Dancers, a performing dance group, and is a volunteer counselor at the Pregnancy and Family Care Center in Leesburg, Florida.

A member of The Florida Authors & Publishers Association (FAPA), Florida Writers Association (FWA), the Writers League of The Villages (WLOV), and Associate Member of the Academy of American Poets, Barbara has a Bachelor of Science degree in Home Economics and Education from West Virginia Wesleyan College and a Master of Arts degree in Family Studies from Montclair State University in N.J.

Barbara lives in The Villages, Florida with her husband Michael Yankus. She has three children, four stepchildren and eighteen grandchildren.

Contact her at Barbaratwoten@gmail.com

Or on her website at www.DancesOfLifePoetry.com

About the Illustrator

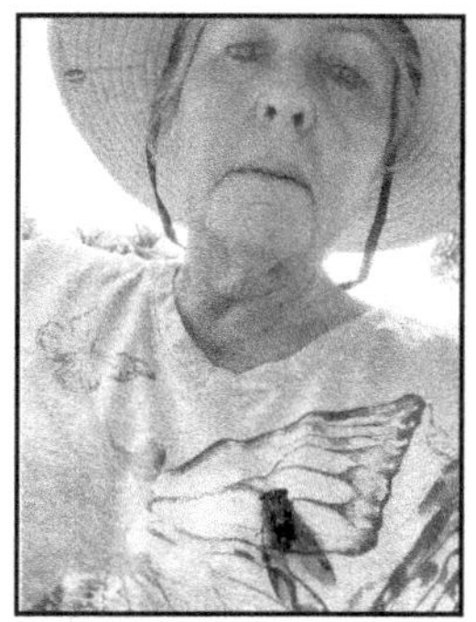

Dr. Catharine Mannion, friend, fellow dancer, and dog-lover grew up in southern California and eventually ended up in Florida. She is a Professor Emeritus from the University of Florida, Department of Entomology and Nematology. She has a Ph.D. from University of Florida in Entomology, a M.S. from North Carolina State University in Entomology, and a B.S. in Biology from University of California, Davis.

In her career her focus has been research and extension (outreach) in which she worked towards solving the many problems of invasive pests. Her work in Florida encompassed biology and management of new and established invasive pests affecting ornamental plants. She truly loves the exciting world of bugs and other creepy crawlers and their environments, and enjoys sharing this beautiful world with others.

Catharine was always creative and enjoyed using these talents in her various presentations of her research. She was always a bit of a "doodler" but found she had a gift she could share through her drawings. It started with a few drawings of insects for fellow entomologists and friends as gifts and cards and grew to specific sketch requests.

She is completely self-taught and primarily works in pencil and ink but has been spreading her wings in watercolor. She hopes to continue sharing her artwork because it brings her so much joy to not only create these works, but to share them!

Catharine currently lives in Ocala, FL, with her two dogs, Paco, and Oscar.

Contact her at: cmm8922@gmail.com

www.ingramcontent.com/pod-product-compliance
Lightning Source LLC
Chambersburg PA
CBHW061308210726
48293CB00003B/1170